The Curse

of

Addy McMahon

by Katie Davis

Greenwillow Books

An Imprint of HarperCollins *Publishers*

The Curse of Addy McMahon
Copyright © 2008 by Katie Davis

All rights reserved. Printed in the United States of America. No part of this book may be used or reproduced in any manner whatsoever without written permission except in the case of brief quotations embodied in critical articles and reviews. For information address HarperCollins Children's Books, a division of HarperCollins Publishers, 1350 Avenue of the Americas, New York, NY 10019.
www.harpercollinschildrens.com

The text of this book is set in Adobe Caslon.
Book design by Victoria Jamieson

Library of Congress Cataloging-in-Publication Data
Davis, Katie (Katie I.)
The curse of Addy McMahon / by Katie Davis.
p. cm.
"Greenwillow Books."
Summary: After her father's death, aspiring sixth-grade writer Addy McMahon feels like she is cursed with bad luck, and when she temporarily loses her best friend, and is forced to admit that her mother is dating again, she vows she will never write another word.
ISBN 978-0-06-128711-4 (trade bdg.) —
ISBN 978-0-06-128712-1 (lib bdg.)
[1. Authorship—Fiction. 2. Cartoons and comics—Fiction. 3. Grief—Fiction. 4. Family life—Fiction. 5. Friendship—Fiction. 6. Behavior—Fiction.] I. Title.
PZ7.D2944Cu 2008
[Fic]—dc222007041154

First Edition 10 9 8 7 6 5 4 3 2 1

 Greenwillow Books

Dedicated to the dedicated
Elizabeth Harding
xo

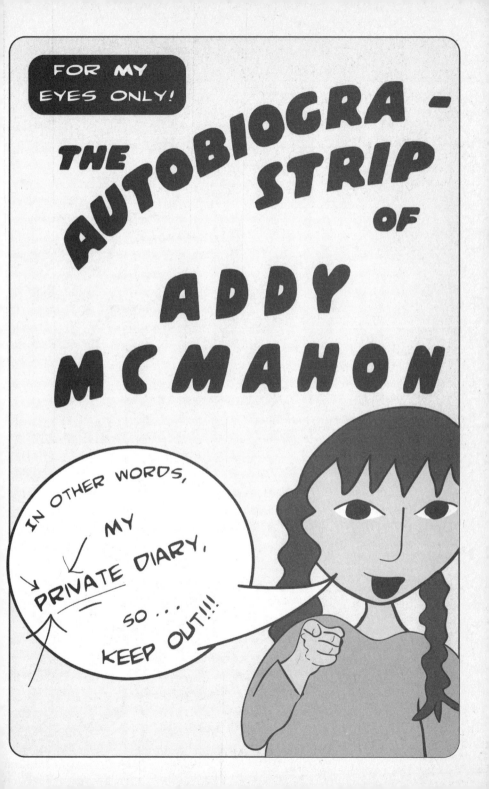

"**C'mon,** Addy, what's the use of being a best friend if you don't get to share secrets?" Jackie asked. "Pleeeeeeeease show me what you're writing?"

"I'm only drawing. Why don't you just finish your math homework?" I said. I stepped over Jackie's books and papers, which were scattered in a semi-circle on my floor. I flopped down on the bed and started sketching my next page.

"Is that your autobio . . . autobi . . . autobiography strip?"

"Wait." I tore a page out of my pad, scribbled a cheat sheet, and Frisbeed it down to the floor. As she picked it up and started to read, I said, "Repeat after me: auto-bi-aw-gra-strip."

Jackie sailed the paper back to me and said, "Very funny." She stood up and leaned over, try-ing to see what I

autobiography + comic strip = autobiogra-strip!
PRONOUNCE:
auto → [drawing of car]
bi → "by" Addy McMahon
aw → isn't it AWful that I won't show you?!
gra → rhymes with DRAW
strip [drawing of comic strip panels]

was working on. "Let me look at it anyway."

I curled my arm around my notebook and asked, "Do *you* let me see *your* diary?"

"That's different, Addy."

"Just because my journal is like a comic strip and yours isn't?"

Jackie harrumphed. "Exactly! The pictures make it nothing like mine, and you're probably the first kid ever in the history of kids who had a graphic diary. So it's no fair you're not sharing! C'mon, you know how much I love a good comic book."

I could tell it was killing her since Jackie didn't like to miss out on anything, which was why she was so terrible about surprises. Every year she found her birthday gifts and peeked. She was fantastic at rewrapping. We weren't even on holiday break yet, and she'd already searched her house and found six Christmas presents. Without thinking, I looked over at a package on my shelf, and she followed my eyes.

It was about the size of our math textbook, wrapped in red-and-white-striped paper. I'd tied about a million mini candy canes on green ribbons, and they dangled from the package like wind chimes. Jackie *loved* candy canes. Which is why I wrapped her present like that.

"Who's that for?" she asked, jumping up and reaching for the package. I was faster, though, and grabbed it, making the candy canes click together.

"No one. It isn't for you . . . yet!" I said, dashing into the hall with Jackie right behind me. But I got to my mom's room with enough time to stash it under a pile of blankets on a chair in the corner. I turned around to find Jackie standing in the doorway, arms crossed, craning her neck to see behind me. We both knew she'd never go searching through my mom's room, so for now, at least, that was one Christmas present she wouldn't get until December twenty-fifth.

We went back into my room, and I picked up my autobiogra-strip. "And this isn't for public viewing either, but I will tell you this," I said. "My mom and I were at Lovely Ladies, buying something I didn't even need, so why was I there in the first place, and

Marsha Pit*tel* Like French walked in and saw."

"Addy," Jackie scolded.

"What? I'm just saying what she always says. 'It's Pit*tel*, like French'!" I didn't know what the problem was. I sounded exactly like Marsha.

I couldn't figure out why it wasn't obvious to everyone that Marsha Pittel was *the* most obnoxious girl in our entire class. *I* could see it the day she moved here in the middle of fourth grade and started taking over practically everything.

Each day at recess all the kids played kickball and I was the best, even if I do say so. Ezra Samuels and Leon Ravets were fantastic, but I could skunk them, too. Then Marsha moved in and she was really good. No matter how hard I tried to get her out, I missed, and missed, and missed again. Everyone wanted her on their side. To top it all off, Marsha joined the Tigers, *my* soccer team since kindergarten.

It was bad enough to be in the same classroom, listening to her show off every single vocabulary word she knew or watching her go to the blackboard to do a math problem in six seconds flat. And she never even erased anything. That's just freakish. But when she started playing on *my* soccer team, I had to quit. I didn't need to be her teammate, too.

That was the first year the Tigers ever went to the championships.

"Anyway," Jackie said, "could that be your worst nightmare, or what? Nothing like your biggest enemy watching your mom buy you your first bra."

"Hey! How'd you know it was a bra?"

Jackie laughed. "You said it was something you didn't need!"

"Ha. Ha. Ha," I said, and flicked my pen at her.

"At least you got to go to Lovely Ladies. They have the nicest stuff around," Jackie said.

"You are such a fashionista."

"Hey, can I help it if I happen to be stylin'?" She put one hand on her waist and the other at the back of her head, wiggled her hips around, and struck a pose.

"Yep, you're the real thing," I said as Jackie fanned herself with her hand.

"I *am* hot, and I don't mean temperature-wise."

"She even tried to crack a lame joke," I said.

"Who did?" Jackie asked, plopping back down on the floor.

"Marsha! She said, 'Why is your mom buying your brother a bra?' Like it was so small only a boy would wear it. Even though, you know, boys don't—"

"I *know* what she meant. What did you say?" Jackie stacked her homework in a neat pile and started to slide everything into her backpack.

"Nothing. I left and waited for my mom by the car."

"No," Jackie said. "I mean, what did you say to her first? About her name?"

"I have absolutely no idea what you're talking about."

"Hello? Let me introduce myself—I'm Jackie, your best friend, and I know you better than anyone. What'd you say?" She looked at me expectantly, then held her hand up, waving it in the air. "No, wait, let me guess. Something like, 'Hi, Marsha, are you taking your dog for a *piddle*?' or 'The bathroom's in the back if you want to, you know, *piddle*.'"

"Well, it's not like Marsha Pit*tel* has ever done

anything but ruin my life, and seeing my bra-buying humiliation just proves again that I'm cursed."

Jackie crumpled up a piece of paper and threw it at my head. "How many times do I have to say it? You. Are. Not. Cursed."

I stuck my tongue out at her. "How many times do I have to tell *you* the stories where my nana has seen total proof? Like when she was leaving for her big job interview at Drive-U-Crazy Driving School and her car wouldn't start? And what about the day she was eating at the diner and her false teeth fell out and the waiter stepped on them? She said she went straight to her dentist, but when she got there all she found was a sign that said he'd quit to open a candy store. Nana always tells how she walked around saying, 'I'm curthed' until she could find a new dentist."

I waited until Jackie stopped laughing. "Anyway, it could be true. You never know," I told her.

"She's *joking*. You know, the kind of joke where you roll your eyes, like you're admitting you know the stuff you're saying isn't really funny? Except for that '*I'm curthed*' part. That cracks me up every time." She sat on the edge of my bed and looked over my shoulder as I drew a new picture of Marsha.

"That is just gross," Jackie said.

"Hey! No peeking, but yeah, she is. I don't know how you can stand it, being co-editors on *The Seely Times* together."

"No, Addy, *that* is gross!" She pointed to my dresser, where a plate sat, full of what used to be food, now growing something green and fuzzy. "What is it?"

"I read somewhere that fairies like human food, so I always leave a Plate of Appeasement, just in case."

Jackie asked, "Appee—*what?*"

"Appeasement. It's like, to calm someone down. If I appease the fairies, maybe they'll lift the curse," I explained. I didn't know what they'd like, but to be safe I included a selection from all the major food groups: Oreos, gummi worms, and cookie dough. You can never go wrong with cookie dough. Unless, of course, you leave it out for a month. Now it just looked like a science experiment gone wrong.

I said, "Sheesh clabeesh, I hope the fairies don't get even madder."

Jackie stood up and heaved one of her famous sighs. "You are impossible."

I put the notebook away and picked up my brush, but had no luck when I tried to drag it through my hair. "Anyway, Jackie, if I weren't cursed my dad wouldn't have died, probably."

Jackie grabbed the brush and sat behind me on my bed, like we did during sleepovers. She started on the knots at the bottom and worked her way up. "He died because he had a cancer, not a curse. You have more tangles in your head than you do in your hair, Addy."

"I should've told him he had to stop smoking or I wouldn't be his daughter anymore. Maybe he'd still be alive now."

Jackie said, "My mom always says that's a useless way to think because people do what they really want to do anyway." Jackie put the brush down and held out her hand. I put two hair thingies in her palm, and she started braiding. "Like, you keep saying you want to be published, but I doubt it or you would've entered the *Chanticleer* contest by now."

"I do too. I just don't want my favorite magazine on the entire planet to tell me I stink."

"If your interviews stunk, why would the mayor send you a fan letter after you wrote about her? C'mon, it's your life's dream. You're never going to get published in a real magazine if you don't send it in, and the deadline gets closer every day."

There was a knock and my brother Nicky burst in. "Mom wants you to set the table for dinner before Jonathan gets here!"

I crossed my eyes and scrunched my nose at Jackie and whispered, "Ugh. Jonathan's coming over for dinner."

Nicky said, "I heard that, Addy, and Mom is right. You *are* stubborn." He ran back out.

"Just like Daddy was," I hollered after him.

Jackie winced. "Do you have to scream right in my face?"

"Heh-heh. Sorry." Then to Nicky I yelled, "Wait a second. How am I being stubborn?"

Jackie covered her ears with her hands, trying not to let go of my hair at the same time. "Addy! Cut it out or I won't ever do your braids again as long as you live."

"Sorry, Jack."

Nicky poked his head back in the room and said, "Because you won't remember that Jonathan's moving in tonight and I know it's on purpose so that means you're stubborn!"

"See, Jackie?" I whispered. "Having Jonathan in my life *proves* I've got a curse."

I'd just set the table and was about to finish my homework when my mother walked into the kitchen, wiping glue from her hands onto her old jeans.

"Hey, Mom. You been working?"

"Yep, Nicky and I were in the Closet," she said.

She was talking about her art room. My dad had been a carpenter, and he broke through the wall separating two huge closets, put up shelves, and built a work island on wheels. It was supposed to be a wedding gift, but Daddy always said, "The carpenter's wife never has shoes." I think it was supposed to be a cobbler, not a carpenter, but my dad had a weird sense of humor. He finally built it for her the same summer he made my frame.

My mom began her design business in that room. Mostly she created collaged invitations and stationery with stuff she found at yard sales, but sometimes she got private commissions. The whole thing started with a huge collection of old comic books she got at a garage sale from some guy who had bought them online, hoping they'd be first editions so he

21

could make a million bucks. They ended up being worthless. That is, until Mom got hold of them. She collaged a gigantic new comic out of hundreds of old ones, added her own speech bubbles written on different kinds of handmade papers, and sold the piece to a gallery in town. That's when I started drawing my own comics.

"I wanted to make Jonathan something for his move-in day," Mom told me over her shoulder as she washed her hands. "I meant to have it done already, but I've been so busy preparing his room, I completely forgot." She turned around and leaned against the sink as she dried off with one of the nubby dish towels. Motioning toward the table, she said, "Addy, you only set three places. Jonathan's eating with us. And you forgot the napkins, honey."

I always forget the napkins. It's a character flaw or something. I put out another setting, went to the cabinet, grabbed three—no, four—napkins, and tucked them under the forks. It's not like Nicky ever uses his napkin anyway. But that's another story. Kind of a gross one.

"Nicky," Mom said as she turned to my brother. He was at the table now, sitting on his knees, hunched over the newspaper. "You need to change into some clean clothes, honey. Something paint-free."

He didn't even look up to answer her. "Wait! Wait! I think we're gonna have a snowstorm soon," he said. "A school-stopper!"

"Nicky," Mom said, her voice rising at the end in that no-TV-later-if-you-don't-listen-to-me-now tone.

I warned him, "Since you're the only nine-year-old *ever* who actually watches The Weather Channel you better listen, or who's going to give all your little buddies the forecast for the next twenty-four hours?"

Nicky looked at me like I was the biggest dope in the universe. He said, "The Weather Channel isn't all forecasts, duh, Addy. There're programs, too, like *Storm Stories*, and *Epic Conditions*, and *It Could Happen Tomorrow*."

"What could happen tomorrow?" I asked him.

He leaned to his right to see past me and said

loudly, looking at Mom, "I don't know because I'm not allowed to stay up that late so even if it *could* happen tomorrow, I wouldn't be ready for it because I don't even know what *it* is!"

"I know what could happen tomorrow," Mom said. "You could lose your TV privilege if you don't go and get changed right now." She poked the air with her thumb, pointing upstairs. Nicky gasped and ran for his room.

After he left, Mom looked at me and chuckled. "'A school-stopper,'" she repeated, and shook her head, still smiling. She came over and gave me a one-armed hug. I buried my nose into her side and inhaled that scent of freshly washed laundry. I don't know how she always smelled like that even when she'd been in the Closet, or gardening all day. "I'm going to get dressed myself, honey. If you hear someone at the door, let me know, okay?"

No way I wanted to hang around, listening for Jonathan's knock like I couldn't wait till he arrived. I ran upstairs, flung my door open, and took a flying leap onto my bed, making all my old stuffed animals jump like they were surprised to see me.

I started a new chapter in my autobiogra-strip about how my life would be so much better if my great-grandad hadn't existed. I guess I wouldn't even be alive if that were true, but if I had one wish, I'd change the history of my family so that everything would be different now.

It all started when my great-grandad chopped down a tree near Latoon, Ireland. From that moment on, my family has had nothing but luck. The bad kind.

It turned out it wasn't just a tree, the one great-grandad chopped. It was a fairy lair. At least that's what all the people around Latoon believed. It was a place where fairies hang out, I guess, or something like that.

The first bit of bad luck happened right away. You have to understand, my great-grandad was a farmer, so the guy had to know how to chop a tree. But this one, the one that everyone thought was a fairy lair, it came falling down the *wrong way*. The people who were there all said it was impossible because there was no wind. But down it came, backward, took him by surprise, conked him right on the head, and he fell, dead. Just like the tree. Everyone who saw it happen ran to him, even though they could tell he was a goner. When they got closer, it looked as though the branches were holding him, like arms, blocking his escape.

The tree had a huge wound caused by the axe and they said something white—like sap, but not sap—oozed out of the middle. It had the consistency of blood. *Fairy blood.*

Nana remembered the scar her mother carried from that day where she got stabbed by a branch. When Great-grandma Annie saw what had happened, she ran to her husband and threw herself on him, ignoring the tree pinning him to the ground, and got a gash in her shoulder. Great-grandma Annie would have lain there forever, crying out of fear and grief, but the townspeople pulled her off Great-grandad and brought her home to tend to her wound. Nana said the scar was shaped like an axe.

I've never been to Ireland, and all my relatives left

right after great-grandad destroyed the fairy lair. But my nana told me this story a million times, so I can practically see the place in my mind like I've lived there my whole twelve years. I've always imagined it before the whole chopping thing. It wasn't so much a tree as a tall shrub with a thick trunk. The branches kind of reached to the left, like they were trying to grab something, or the wind was blowing them. But that's just the way it grew.

Most people probably don't believe in fairies. They think, How can you have fairies in a world with stuff like cell phones, the Internet, sheep cloning, and science and everything?

But if it *is* true that fairies curse you when you cross them, then what happens to someone who chops down their home and causes a fairy massacre? He probably gets a ginormous King Kong curse, that's what. The chopper gets it, and so does his great-granddaughter.

"**C'mon,** Addy, I want you to see this!" Mom hollered up the stairs.

I ran down as she marched into the kitchen, dressed in her favorite blue flannel skirt and a long-sleeved white T-shirt. She never wore her hair down, but now it was combed and swung at her shoulders. Nicky trailed after her. They each clutched the corner of a giant sign that they lay in the middle of the kitchen floor because it was too big for the table. It read, "Welcome home!" in bright pink paint. A checkered border edged the top and bottom. I could smell the Magic Marker Nicky used to draw the little black and red squares. Blue and yellow flowers were painted all over the sign, falling into the letters and littering the bottom of the words, partly hiding them.

Welcome home? That was for people who went away and came back. And once Jonathan found another apartment, he could *stay* away. After Daddy's funeral, our family did feel lopsided with only the three of us. But it's not like he could be replaced just so we could have an even four.

Before I could help myself, I rolled my eyes. And Mom saw.

"Addy."

I knew that tone.

"Sorry, Mom, but 'welcome home'? It's not like he's staying or anything." I glanced at the picture of my dad that sat on the hutch. If Daddy were here, there'd be no Jonathan around. Mom caught me looking at the photo, and her expression changed.

She stepped over the sign, sat next to me at the table, and took my hand. "If you'd stop being so stubborn and give him a chance, you'd see that Jonathan might be a good thing in your life. I *know* he's good for me." With her free hand she tucked a clump of her dark hair behind her ear, and I could see she hadn't gotten all the glue off her fingers.

I also saw that her wedding ring was gone.

There was an uneven pounding, and Mom rushed to go open the door. Standing there was a gigantic stack of boxes being held by a tall someone.

Before anyone could say anything, Mom ran back out of the room.

I could see a bald head trying to look from behind the teetering tower. "Hi, Addy, uh, ow . . ." Jonathan peeked from behind the cartons. I heard him grunting as he balanced the heavy load. Then he took a step into the house and called out like some goofy old TV show, "Honey! I'm home!"

My mom and Nicky came marching out from the kitchen holding the welcome banner and singing a dumb song about home sweet home.

Mom practically squealed. "I can't *believe* you said 'Honey I'm home!' Look at this!" She and Nicky held the sign high, covering their faces.

Jonathan readjusted his load and started laughing. "I guess great minds really do think aliiiii— ah!" The boxes tipped out of his arms, spilling papers all over the place.

Mom peeked from behind the banner and groaned. "Oh, hon, I'm so sorry! All your work . . . oh, no . . ." She turned to Nicky and said, "Let's set the sign down . . . give me your corners, that's it."

They brought their hands together like two people folding a sheet. She took the end he'd been holding and, matching the edges, quickly rolled up the banner and stood it in the corner. Dropping to her knees, she started gathering the spilled papers, but Jonathan stopped her.

"No, no, it's okay, Cassie," Jonathan said, squatting down. "I'll get it. It's my fate. Each time I avoid weeding through everything, the universe forces me to do something about it."

"I thought you didn't believe in fate," Mom said.

"I don't. Except when it interferes." Jonathan reached for a folder my mom was holding out to him. He tried to take it from her, but she wouldn't let go. He tugged on it. She tugged back. Jonathan smiled at her and my mom giggled. Totally G-ross.

I couldn't take it anymore and walked out of the room, stepping over some of Jonathan's papers. He's a freelance writer. "I never know who's going to sign my next paycheck," he always says, and then laughs, even though it's not even funny. Basically he works for lots of different people and not just for one company. He's written books, and articles, and columns for magazines and newspapers.

But he's not just a writer. No, Jonathan's an *interviewer*. That's his specialty. When I first met him and he found out I was famous for *my* interviews, he practically had a cow. Ever since then, it seemed like every conversation we had was all about Jonathan giving me his writing *tips*. Or as I called them, *insults*.

"So, Addy," he'd said, "I read some of the newsletters you've been doing. I like how the interviews have illustrations—like a picture book. Not bad. Maybe someday you can be a published writer, like me."

"I *am* published," I had told him. *Not bad?* How about *really great?!* Lots of people *loved* my newsletters. I'd been writing them for over a year by then. I knew what I was doing.

"No, I mean, well, yes," he went on, "you're published. It's great that your teacher helps you print and distribute them—"

"Throughout the entire town, you know," I interrupted.

"Yes," Jonathan had said, "and that's great. But if you work on your writing, you'll have a craft that can take you anywhere. You could get paid to write, and travel all around the world. You're welcome to read the interviews I do. Maybe you'd get some ideas."

I never did take him up on that offer. I already had plenty of my own ideas.

Now he was standing in the middle of the mess he'd just made. "C'mon, Addy," he called. "Now's your chance to see all my work at one time!"

That was Jonathan being really funny. "Can't hear you . . . water's running," I hollered from the kitchen.

He walked in with a box full of messed-up papers and books. He leaned it on the edge of the counter and looked through it, pulling out a thin paperback with curled edges, like he'd thumbed through it so many times, the pages recoiled from his touch.

"Oh, look, here's one of my old style guides. They're great for learning the correct way to write," he said.

I reached up to get the glasses out of the cabinet and looked at him. "I write what I want to write. No one's complained yet." I turned the faucet on and filled the glasses, then got milk for Nicky and me.

"You sure? You'll learn more than you can guess." When I didn't answer, he shrugged and lugged the box upstairs to his room.

I didn't need his help. I started doing my interviews all on my own after I had to quit soccer. I missed playing so much I began hanging around the sidelines. Coach finally yelled at me, "Would you stop with all the questions? At least wait till after the game to interview me."

So I did. I talked to the coaches, and the captains. I spoke to our key players (except Marsha, of course) and then, before the playoffs, I interviewed the team that was up against the Tigers. I wrote all the facts, but I did it so you felt like you were reading a storybook. I didn't even think about publishing it anywhere. It was just fun to tell the story. I drew pictures of people next to their comments, and clouds of dust poofing over the two teams with lots of arms and legs sticking out.

My favorite part was trying to think of different ways to describe a scene, and when I showed it to my teacher, Mrs. Crimi, she had asked, "What did it feel like when you went for a goal and missed the ball completely?" She wondered what the field smelled like, and the fall air, and the dirt when you gouged the ground after a badly aimed kick. Her questions gave me the idea to rewrite it and put in stuff like how cold your hands got during October games, or what it felt like to fly through the air and fall on your butt in front of absolutely everyone. When it was all done, Mrs. Crimi asked if I minded if she made copies so she could brag about her talented student to a bunch of teachers she knew.

Her friends showed it to their friends, and pretty soon it made its way to the school where the other team went. Then their coach called our principal asking for permission to give a copy to every kid. Everyone was reading my story. Reading *my* words.

After that, whenever I could, I put out a newsletter featuring a star interview. Mrs. Crimi helped me publish them, and by the third issue, I was scanning in my art, and making the whole thing digitally. I always included a drawing of the interviewee, and a little box, which I found out was called a sidebar, with the same questions every month. People started comparing the answers in the sidebar, like who was a dog person versus people who loved cats; who hated broccoli and who would eat gross things like snails. (And by the way, being a journalist is great because you find out that there are very weird people who actually do eat stuff like snails. G-ross!)

When I started getting phone calls from people I didn't even know, asking me to interview them, my mom got caller ID. When we moved up to sixth grade, Jackie and I decided to create a newspaper, named after our school. We called it *The*

Seely Times, and asked Mrs. Crimi to be our advisor. Unfortunately, she made us form a whole staff. She said if just the two of us did it alone, we'd never get any homework done. I didn't see the problem, but we got a bunch of other kids involved anyway. We made Ezra and Leon special contributors, and they reported on sports and school events. At first Jackie and I were the co-editors. But since I was also doing the interview column, Mrs. Crimi made me stick to one thing, and just to show how bad my family curse is, Marsha Pittel got to be co-editor with Jackie.

"You know what the Platinum Pencil is?" Jonathan asked, startling me out of my thoughts. I hadn't even heard him walk back into the kitchen.

"A really expensive writing tool?" I answered. I hoped he wasn't going to start up with his stupid tips.

"It's the name of a writing award for excellence in journalism. Well, turns out I have tickets for this year's bash, and you guys are coming as my guests. Everyone in the magazine industry will be there. Even people from kids' magazines."

Now he was talking about something interesting. "Really? Which ones?"

"I don't know, but if it's a well-respected literary journal, the editorial staff will be there. The Platinum Pencil is a very prestigious award, and no one misses the big night," Jonathan said.

My mom came in and pulled on some blue oven mitts. "Actually, this year Jonathan's the recipient." She checked the oven and frowned. "I forgot to turn this thing on in all the excitement. I'll call for pizza." She picked up the phone and smiled at Jonathan, nudging his arm. "It's very impressive. You should brag more."

"Awards are okay, I guess," I said. "But I'm going to be published because my work comes from the heart, not because I'm trying to win some prize."

"You're being published?" Jonathan looked surprised. "Why didn't you say so?"

"First of all," I said, "I already *am* published . . . every time *The Seely Times* comes out, remember?"

Jonathan nodded his head. "I know, Addy. I just meant—"

"You meant it wasn't real," I told him.

"Of course it's real. It's real practice, and it gives you invaluable experience. I think you have great potential, and I want to see you tap it and grow, that's all. You know, sometimes an award can further your career, and I hope that will happen for me, but that isn't why I write either."

I started to say, "And second of all, if I won the *Chanticleer* contest—"

"Aren't you the one who didn't care about prizes?" Jonathan asked. He raised his bushy eyebrows and smiled like he caught me.

"That's not the same thing," I said, not willing to admit it really kind of was. But he thought he was so great, winning that writing award. I bet I could win the *Chanticleer* contest. All I had to do was enter. That sure would show him.

On the other hand, what if they said I stunk? They were professionals, and they'd know what they were talking about. I'd have to quit writing. Then what would I do?

Nah, I'd totally win. Didn't everyone always say

my interviews were the best? Why else would they keep calling me, asking to be my next subject?

Jonathan droned on and on. It was his usual "try different styles of writing, Addy, you'll learn so much," and "a writer needs a thick skin; there's so much rejection and criticism." I kind of zoned out, staring at the reflection of the ceiling light dancing around on his forehead, which really was his whole head, since most of his hair was gone. The only thing I could find even close to appealing about Jonathan were his dimples. They were really deep and long and he even had them when he talked, not just when he smiled. Jonathan always looked as though he had a little grin on his face, making his eyes all crinkly and kind, but that didn't make me like him any better.

". . . well, I better go put this stuff away before the pizza gets here. You know, Addy, come to think of it, maybe you shouldn't try a different style. Stick to what you're comfortable with. Who knows, maybe you'll find a different creative outlet that you like even more."

What, like I'm settling for less because I want to do things my own way? My dad never had a problem with what I wrote. That's why, when I asked if I could interview him, he put up with about a million questions, even though he was sick. I had to do a bunch of mini interviews, because by then he wasn't strong enough to do it all at once.

He told me about the first time he made up "The Dragon Knight," the story I'd heard all my life. I was about three hours old, and everyone in the hospital, including Mom, was asleep but my dad and me. He described the greenish glow of the fluorescent lights spilling into our room, and imagined a dragon hovered outside the door, ready to pounce. He had scooped me up and cradled me in his arms, and even bundled in a million baby blankets I still felt lighter than a container of milk. In the quiet of that hospital he whispered the story of the knight who protected the little princess from the evil dragon.

I'd grown up listening to him tell "The Dragon Knight," so by the time we had that first interview session, it felt like my story too. That's when we decided to make a comic book of it together. Daddy wrote it, and I illustrated, and it ended up being the first comic I ever made.

Then, when I'd shown him the first draft of the interview, he'd said, "Addy, you are going to be such a great writer someday. In fact, you already are a great writer. Of interviews, that is. Your handwriting could use some work, though." He thought that was hysterical. "Your writing is great, monkey-pushkey, but your writing stinks!"

I did the last interview session with Daddy in late winter, right before he died. I'd been working on it ever since, knowing that someday it would be polished enough to enter the annual *Chanticleer* contest. I had been so busy rewriting and editing the interview that finally it was almost perfect. But the thought kept creeping in . . . what if my favorite magazine on the entire planet said I was terrible? I tried not to think about that. I tried to remember that all the entries were just stories, and no one ever did anything different or inventive. If I submitted an interview in my storybook style, I

47

was sure that something so unique would impress the judges, and if the writing was good on top of that, I definitely had a chance to win.

Winning the contest was a huge big deal. You got a scholarship toward a writing program at the local college, *and* you got published. The second- and third-place winners got big prizes too, like computers and stuff. And even if you lost, your name and the title of your story appeared on their Web site.

But my time was running out. Not only was the deadline zooming closer, but they also changed the rules, and now you couldn't enter if you were older than twelve. This was my last chance to win the contest, and to make sure my dad would be remembered forever and ever.

I shook my head to try to clear it. It's not like I had to decide that instant. After all, Daddy's interview was *this close* to being ready to submit. I could mail it at the last minute, which left plenty of time between now and then. Thinking about the deadline reminded me I needed to start on my next interview for the *Times*.

From: writergurl@mac.com

Subject: our next issue

To: jackierainbow@mac.com

jack,

wanna be my next interview subject? after the mayor, 3 teachers and the principal its time i did a kid. anyway youre the best choice.

from me

From: jackierainbow@mac.com

Subject: re: our next issue

To: writergurl@mac.com

SURE!!! COOL!!!! BUT WHY ME?

o srry didnt mean 2 scream @ u. hahahahahahaha

From: writergurl@mac.com

Subject: re: re: our next issue

To: jackierainbow@mac.com

DUH youre popular and all that garbage. no offense. haha

PS lets do it after school tomorrow

From: jackierainbow@mac.com

Subject: re: re: re: our next issue

To: writergurl@mac.com

ok seriously now . . . its nice, Ad, but i dont think it would be fair for the editor of the paper to be an interview subject. it seems weird like im conceited or something.

From: writergurl@mac.com

Subject: re: re: re: re: our next issue

To: jackierainbow@mac.com

i see what u mean. but rlly jackie, u run the school paper and kids want 2 know how its done. maybe you could (you wont believe this is me talking!) let marsha be the only editor on this edition. no thats too horrible to imagine. how about just on the interview?? we wont let u c it before publication just like any other interviewee. and we could put that in a sidebar to explain.

As I waited for her to answer, I wondered how she'd be able to resist reading it. Jackie'd have to fight the double-whammy temptation of acting like the editor *and* being the subject of the interview. She took her job very seriously, but Jackie was Jackie, which meant she *had* to know everything that was going on. We'd just have to keep her from reading it, and that was that.

From: jackierainbow@mac.com
Subject: re: re: re: re: re: our next issue
To: writergurl@mac.com

its a deal. c ya!!!!

Now that that was settled, I made a promise to myself that once I was done with this assignment, I'd finish the very last stuff on my dad's piece and send it off to *Chanticleer*. After I won the contest, I'd be famous for my great interview style and creative approach, and not just in my own town. It would finally prove to Jonathan, once and for all, that I could write any way I wanted.

After school Jackie and I walked straight to my house. We gobbled some snacks in the kitchen, went up to my room, and settled on my floor. I put the tape recorder between us and leaned back against my bed.

"Okay, ready?" I pushed the Play and Record buttons at the same time and through the window of the old plastic machine, the tape began to roll. I said, "Jackie White, by Addy McMahon."

Me: What is your name and age?

Jackie: Jackie and I'm twelve years old.

Me: You are the editor of this paper, so how can you be the subject of a feature interview? How can you make sure it will be honest and fair?

Note to self—describe Jackie's: —curly brown hair —brown hazely eyes like a Sugar Daddy only not sticky ha ha simile or metaer? metaphor

55

Jackie: I am not the editor of this piece, and have vowed not to read it before it's published.

(I tried not to laugh here, but I couldn't help it!)

Jackie: What? I *could* have willpower if I wanted to, you know, Addy.

Me: Who is your best friend?

Jackie: Duh.

Me: We have to do this official, you know. I'm just making sure you're giving me honest answers.

Jackie: You don't think I can have willpower? I—

Me: I do, I do. Just answer, okay? C'mon.

Jackie: Fine. You, Addy McMahon, are my best friend since forever.

We talked for so long we used up the first side of the tape. I flipped it over and asked her a couple more questions, but it seemed sort of stupid, since we'd known each other since tricycles. But you never know when you're going to find out something new, so I just pretended like Jackie was a regular interview subject.

Me: Who else is on your favorite person list?

Jackie: You know.

OMG! Jackie totally blushed here!

I don't say anything. Like a real reporter, you have to wait till the other person says stuff so you don't get into the interview yourself.

Jackie: Okay, fine. Ezra Samuels. Hey Addy, do you think Ezzie likes me? You know Mrs. Metro warned him that just because he and Leon are best friends doesn't make them ideal lab partners, and now I think he might have asked her if he could be my lab partner instead. That would be so awesome. Maybe we could go to the sixth-grade dance together. You don't think he'd kiss me, do you?

I don't say anything again. When Jackie starts talking about Ezra Samuels, she barely takes a breath. The girl doesn't know when to quit. And anyway, *g-ross*! Kissing Ez? Even though Ezra was definitely the cutest boy in our grade, and Leon wasn't far behind, Jackie and I never really cared about that because the four of us had known each other since preschool and once you've practically been in diapers with a boy, he kind of seems like your brother instead of a real boy. I can't even imagine wanting to kiss anyone, and Jackie was talking about kissing Ez? Ew. Ew. Ew. But apparently Jackie had forgotten all about preschool and being *my* best friend and all she wanted to do was talk about Ezra and think about Ezra and hang out with Ezra.

Jackie: Hey! You can't write that part!
Me: You have to say "off the record," or I can write anything you say.
Jackie: You better not write that about Ezra or I'll never talk to you again!

She started to run out of my room here, until I promised to never, ever, ever, ever, ever tell anyone

58

that she liked Ezra Samuels. As long as she didn't like him more than she liked me, I agreed.

Jackie put out her palm and said, "Spit shake."

"No way. We haven't done that since kindergarten, and it was disgusting even then."

"Okay, if we don't do that . . ." Jackie said, digging in her pocket for her strawberry lip gloss. She smeared some on her palm and then took my wrist in her hand and squeezed a warm glob onto mine. ". . . then we have to do a blood sister thing."

The fake strawberry scent floated up from my hand, and the glitter in the red gel twinkled as it caught the light.

I said, "Well, at least we didn't have to actually bleed."

"Yeah, this'll work," agreed Jackie. We shook on it and smushed the sparkling lip gloss together, while I swore I wouldn't tell anyone ever ever, ever, ever.

"Hey," she said. "I saw the moving van at your house."

"Yeah, Jonathan brought his stuff over."

"So they're getting married?" Jackie asked. She

drew a smiley face with her fingernail in the gloss glob still on her palm.

I took a tissue and wiped my hand clean. "What are you talking about? Why would you ever think *that*?"

Jackie said, continuing to doodle in the gel, "Duh, Addy. He moved in?"

"Duh yourself. He lost his lease. He'll be looking for a new place and leaving. Very soon. Sheesh, Jackie, my dad only just died."

"It was really sad, Addy, but it's been two years."

"It has only been one year, eight months, and three and a half weeks, okay? It's way too soon for my mom to even date. Or think about dating. Or use the word *date*."

"Or say anything that starts with the letter *D*?" Jackie gave me one of her big drama sighs and said, "You are being so close to clueless, Addy. I know you miss your dad and all, but come on. Why would your mom let Jonathan move in if they didn't have plans or whatever? My cousin lived with his girlfriend before they got married." She kept drawing spirals

60

on her hand in the gloss. It made me want to vomit.

"Would you just wipe that junk off your hand already? This isn't finger painting class, you know!" I tossed the tissue box at her and stood there with my arms crossed. "You think you're so smart, Jackie, but Jonathan's not *living* with us. He's staying in the guest room. Why? Because he's a *guest*. And he'll be a guest until he finds another apartment. That is *all*."

Jackie finished wiping her hands with the tissue, stood up, and dropped it into the trash basket under my desk. "Fine, Addy. Whatever. I gotta go and do my homework."

"Fine."

"Fine."

She picked up her backpack, flung it across her shoulder, and marched out of my room and down the stairs. I heard the front door close a few seconds later.

Normally I wrote my first draft right after speaking to the person because I always got a stronger flavor if I'd just been with them. But I was not in the kind of mood to write something nice about Jackie

White right then. She thought she could tell what was going on, but she didn't live in my house. She didn't know anything at all. Jackie didn't even know how idiotic she sounded when she started talking about Ezra, so how could she possibly imagine what my mom was going to do?

My room was too small, and pacing back and forth only got me madder. I sat down and started drawing instead. Before I knew it, I had a new comic. Too bad I could never let anyone read it.

My mom made me go to this annoying grief counselor after my dad died. She kept trying to get me to hit Bobo the clown, in order to "work out my anger." What*ever*. My buddy Bobo was this big blow-up punching bag with sand sewn in the bottom. Problem was, every time I hit him he just bounced right back up with that stupid grin on his face, breezing me with his plasticky new-doll smell. Made me want to take a pin and pop him.

After I started seeing her, though, my comics changed. Instead of made-up stories, I began doing more stuff that was more private, which is how I came up with autobiogra-strip. Usually you just get to be in a situation once, and whatever you do or say, that's your only chance. But every time I sketched a panel or put together a scene, it was like living it over again. I made a lot of comics about my dad.

I started doing the same process I used with my interviews, scanning in my line art, tracing over that, using different layers, and it all connected in the end. One image is just a still frame, but when you put a whole bunch together, it's like a movie. Every comic was a different clip from my life.

Even though nobody saw them, every time I made one, I didn't feel as bad. It was kind of like when you're sick. After you barf, you feel better.

And it was the same with "The Mental Adventures of Jackie White." Once it was down on paper, I wasn't mad at all.

By the time we finished eating dinner, I was thinking about how much I hated being in a fight with Jackie. It hardly ever happened, and I wasn't used to it. We needed to make up, and I knew just the way to do it. I worked on her interview the rest of the night. Even though it was an early draft, it was really great. I added in some stuff only I would know, like how when we first moved in, and Nicky was very little, he got lost and Jackie found him wandering around the neighborhood. If she hadn't been there, who knows what would've happened? Jackie practically saved his life.

I backed up the interview and opened my e-mail app. I started writing a message to the *Times*'s staff

69

Listserv, reminding them not to show Jackie the document, since it was all about her. But I stopped typing. I bit my nails as I realized if she really didn't read the interview until it was published, how was it going to help us make up? I counted the weeks on my fingers until the next issue of *The Seely Times*. It wouldn't, that's how.

Then I had a great idea. I thought about how good Jackie was at rewrapping packages. I bet if I sent her the interview "by accident" she wouldn't be able to resist opening it up and then how could she *not* read it? If I knew Jackie, she'd just act like nothing happened. But *she* would know what a great piece I'd done *in her honor* and everything would be back to normal between us.

From: writergurl@mac.com
Subject: jackies interview
To: jackierainbow@mac.com
hey fellow times staff members!

it wasnt easy but i finished jackies interview!!!! its pretty good if you ask me. but dont ask me since i'll sound really conceited then. haha.

addy

PS: remember—do NOT show this to jackie, since its ALL about her!

I attached the interview and sent it off to Jackie. She would be reading it before bedtime, I was sure, and by tomorrow, everything would be fine between us.

Boy was I wrong.

The next morning I grabbed my two notebooks, stuffed them into my already full backpack, and clomped down the stairs. I dumped my load on the chair in the kitchen reserved for the soon-to-be recycled newspapers. Everything, including the paper pile, slid off and fell onto the floor.

Nicky burst out laughing. Since he's my brother, of course I ignored him, but he helped me with the mess anyway. I gave him a thumbs-up before he left the kitchen, and he waved his arms around in the air, making crashing sounds and laughing.

I was getting the cereal out when my mom came in dressed in her sweats. Her hair was tied back, even though half of it had come out during her morning run. She always said that her two kids, plus running, were the three things that gave her strength after Daddy died. She smiled at me as she picked up the boxes and put them back in the cabinet.

"I've got a special breakfast planned for us," she said as she went to the stove, pulling on the blue oven mitts. She grabbed the handle of a big black pot spewing steam and, lifting off the lid, tilted it toward me so I could see inside.

"Mac and Cheese and Peas!" I said. Mac and cheese was the only food I'd eat for years when I was little. Then Nicky was born and would only eat what I ate, so my dad always made it with peas, because he wanted us to get something green. Mac and Cheese and Peas was our absolute favorite, partly because Mac and Cheese and Peas is so yummy, but also because we thought it was funny to say.

Mom plopped a huge pile on my plate and my mac mountain oozed toward the edges of the dish. I leaned my face into the tentacles of steam twirling upward and took a deep breath of butter and cheese sauce perfume. Suddenly I was starving. I hadn't eaten too much at dinner the night before. The fight with Jackie, plus Jonathan's arrival, kind of just killed my appetite.

"Mom, how long is Jonathan going to have to stay here, anyway?" I asked, taking a bite. I felt the steam escape my lips, and I tilted my head from side to side, trying not to burn my mouth.

Right then Nicky bounded back into the kitchen and said, "Mom! We had two avalanches in two days! *Paper* avalanches! First Jonathan's and then Addy's!"

I held up my hand to Nicky to get him to be quiet. Turning to my mother, I asked again, "How long?"

But then Jonathan walked in and Mom said, "We'll talk about this later." We were already halfway through breakfast so I knew "later" would be a long wait.

Jonathan tap-tap-tapped a bunch of folders he was holding into a neat stack and set them down on the counter. "I'm finally getting my room settled: half bedroom, half office."

Nicky said, "You could call it your boffice! No, your bedfice . . . how about your—"

"How about I just call it my room?" He ruffled Nicky's hair and smiled.

He'd better not get too settled, I thought.

Jonathan sat down and looked at his own mound of Mac and Cheese and Peas with suspicion.

"Guess what?" Nicky asked. "You had a paper avalanche yesterday and Addy had one today! I bet there's a fault under this house. We've been studying geography and there are cracks in the earth and when they move they—oh, wait. That's for earthquakes. Never mind." He grabbed his spoon like it was a weapon and used it to attack his second helping.

Jonathan just sat there, watching Nicky inhale his food. "*This* is breakfast? What do you eat for dinner, cornflakes?"

My mom set down a steaming cup of coffee in front of him and said, "This is the kids' favorite food from—well, from before. I wanted your first breakfast here to be special." She had that tone grown-ups got when they're trying to tell each other something but they don't want the kids to figure out what it is.

Mom continued, "And besides, what's the difference if you eat it now or later? Even if we did have cornflakes for dinner, it would all still balance, right?"

But she couldn't distract me, *or* fool me. I knew why she made our favorite food. "Mom, do you actually think you can buy me off with a . . . a . . . pile of pasta?"

Nicky said, "I'm eating a p-p-p-pile of p-p-p-pasta!"

and started to laugh, until he saw I wasn't kidding around.

Jonathan looked at Nicky, then back and forth, from me to my mother. He opened his mouth to speak, but closed it, which was a good thing. I definitely didn't want to talk about it with *him*.

"Addy," my mom said, "I'd like to speak to you in private." She walked out of the room and waited for me at the foot of the stairs. "What is going on? What are you talking about, 'buying you off'?"

"You just want everything fine and dandy, and it's *not*. He is the lamest, worst person who ever lived, and you don't think I'm cursed?"

"Addy, please. Enough about that curse," Mom said.

I couldn't believe this. Just because they were all goo-goo, my mom was going to let this guy come and stay in our guest room, and he was what—a part of the family?

She put her hand on my arm. "Addy, Jonathan isn't trying to be your father, you know. No one can take his place, but—"

I shook her off and ran upstairs. I flung myself on my bed and buried my face in the pillow. My old stuffed bunny, Rabbit Jones, fell on my head, like he was trying to give me a hug.

The image of my dad's hands appeared before my closed eyes. He wasn't just a carpenter, he was a craftsman. An *artisan*, my mom always said. He had beautiful hands, like they had been sculpted. Made for creating. I could still smell him. I know that sounds kind of weird, but I imagined myself cuddled up in the crook of his arm while we read our comic, "The Dragon Knight," together. I could hear his voice, all gravely, like he had to clear his throat. And I smelled the faded cigarette smoke mixed in with his aftershave.

I could still hear him say, "Addy, you're going to be such a great writer someday. You already are, but I'm not the only one who will know it." Of course, I can also hear him screaming at me to give his cigarettes back. I always did, but I squeezed the pack first, every time. If I hadn't returned them, maybe he'd still be alive.

I heard someone coming up the stairs. "Addy?"

My mom opened the door and poked her head in.

"What."

She sat on the edge of my bed and crossed her legs. She reached up and took her ponytail down, and when her hair fell forward, she pushed it off her face.

I said, "You took off your ring."

My mother looked at me and then held her right hand over her left, touching the place her wedding band had always been.

"Yes, honey," she said. "There I was, making that welcome home banner for Jonathan, and I realized I was still wearing your father's ring. I mean, the one he gave me."

"For your wedding. Your *marriage*, Mom."

"Yes, Addy, and you know the vow, right? 'Till death do us part'?"

After my dad's funeral, when all the visitors had gone, and we went back to school, it didn't feel right. I kept thinking he could come back—the coast was clear. Like, *Okay, we did that, show's over, you can come out now!* It was very weird. I knew he was dead for real, of course. But "till death do us part," something I'd heard on a million TV shows and even cartoons, never meant anything. Until that moment.

"Anyway," my mom was saying, "ever since Jonathan and I became close, he never once asked me about my ring. He didn't pressure me to take it off, even though it was obvious we were falling in love—"

"Mom!" I said. "That is totally—"

"Addy, please don't interrupt. It's totally natural, is what it is. I loved your father, but he died. Life isn't fair. But life is also giving me another chance at love, and at a whole family." She leaned over and stroked my hair, like I was a baby. My throat closed, and I squeezed my eyes shut.

"Honey, I'm so sorry you and Nicky lost your daddy. He didn't want to go, but he's gone. I'm still here, though, and I love you, my sweet girl." She stood up and went to the door. "I'll tell you one thing. He sure does live on in you. You're just as creative and imaginative as he was." She added with a smile, "Not to mention as stubborn. Now get your rear in gear or you'll be late to school."

I went into the bathroom, splashed some water on my face, and headed down into the kitchen to get my stuff.

Jonathan was still at the table. "You know what I do when I've had a tough morning? I try really hard to pretend it never happened and start fresh."

If only that whole day had never happened. I've had some pretty bad ones so far, but it was right up there in the top five.

If I weren't convinced of a curse before, that day would've done it for me. I tried to run to school, but instead, I kept slipping on all the snow we'd had. And since I *do* live under a curse, I was late because of it. But that's not what clinched it.

When I finally got to school, it took me forever to get to homeroom. First I had to stomp the snow off my boots and pull up a sock that had slipped down off my heel. I was hopping on my other foot when the last bell rang.

I saw Jackie just as I slammed my locker shut and spun my combination lock. If one of us is late, we meet at my locker and walk to homeroom together. I waved and I thought our eyes met, but she must not have seen me because she turned and went the other way.

She was walking with Marsha Pittel. They probably had to talk about the next *Times* issue. But then Marsha linked arms with her, which was so pathetic. Poor Jackie.

Marsha must've trapped her. That's one of the pitfalls of being co-editors, I guessed. I knew Jackie wouldn't want to actually hang out with her on purpose. I started down the hall toward homeroom. I couldn't wait to see her reaction to the interview. She might act like she hadn't read it, so we'd both be in the clear if anyone found out. If she did read it, but didn't want to admit it, I bet she'd just act normal, like we never left on bad terms. On the other hand, it would be fun to hash it over and see what kinds of edits we came up with. We'd have to keep that a secret, though. I hurried, looking forward to laughing together about Marsha getting so chummy.

Everyone was backed up into the hallway, waiting to get in. The logjam finally broke, and I saw Marsha and Jackie head for the last two seats that were next to each other. I guess Jack didn't want to make it too obvious that she was ditching Marsha to sit with me. I had to take the one open desk that was left. Behind them.

Jackie looked over her shoulder at me. I started to say hi when Marsha whispered something to her. She sat so close I thought she was going to sit on Jackie's lap.

I wanted to send her a sympathy signal. "Jackie?" I whispered.

The teacher gave me a dirty look.

I wrote a note and tapped her on the shoulder with it. It worked!

She grabbed it, read what I had written, and gave me the hugest dirty look I'd ever seen in my entire life.

What was going on? Did she read the interview, but hated what I wrote? She had to know it

was just a first draft. Or maybe she figured out that I sent it to her on purpose? That had to be it. She was mad because we agreed she wouldn't read it before publication in order to stay objective. People might not trust an editor who read—and possibly worked on— her own interview. What had I been thinking? She was right to be angry! We'd made a deal, and here I was, trying to tempt her into breaking it. I felt terrible.

After the pledge and roll call we filed back into the hall, and I called for her to wait up. She looked at me as Marsha said to her, "Don't, Jackie. Do you really want to reignite that friendship? It will only magnify everything."

"Oh brother, Marsha," I said. "I can tell you've been studying for our vocab quiz. You better study harder, because you obviously don't know your definitions. You can't *re*ignite something if it hasn't gone out in the first place."

Jackie looked at the ground and kept walking. When I tried to follow her, Marsha stepped in my way. She said, "Oh yeah, right. That's who you are, Miss Innocent." I must've looked confused, because then Marsha said, "Did you learn the word *extinguish* yet? 'Cause that's what you've done to your friendship with Jackie." She threw her backpack on the floor, knelt down, and unzipped the front pocket with a little soccer ball zipper pull.

90

Past the next bank of lockers, Jackie stood clutching her books to her chest and watched from the middle of the hallway.

Marsha pulled out a packet of papers and shoved it in my face. I snarled and grabbed it. When I looked at what I was holding, I thought the mac and cheese from breakfast must've glued all my insides together. I didn't know how I'd ever eat again.

I was holding "The Mental Adventures of Jackie White."

I gasped. "How did you—" It felt like water was filling my lungs. "Why did she—" I couldn't breathe. "I didn't . . . I'm not . . . where did you . . ."

Jackie turned to go.

"Wait!" I called. But she didn't stop. "It was a mistake!" Kids stared as they slammed their lockers shut and ran off before the late bell rang. "It was an accident!" I called to her.

Marsha turned around and hollered back, "Yeah, a big one!" Then she skipped a couple of steps to catch up with Jackie, and the two of them linked arms again to walk off down the hall.

HERE LIES

ADDY

She wasn't that bad.

I barely heard any of my teachers the rest of the day. I could only think about the mess I was in. I wracked my brain as I doodled the word "interview" all over my math workbook. How did Marsha get a copy of "The Mental Adventures of Jackie White"? I never printed it out. How was it even possible?

Maybe someone got into my files? I wasn't sure how the whole wireless thing worked, but I knew someone could just stand outside your house and hack your files. My mom must've put a password on the system, though. So if Marsha didn't do the hacking, then who did? Someone had to have *given* her the comic. Because I knew it definitely couldn't be *my* fault.

For the millionth time, I asked myself the same question: How could this have happened? I checked the attachment. It was called Jackie White Interview.doc. There's no way I would have confused it with "The Mental Adventures of Jackie White."

But if Jackie had gotten hold of the comic first, I couldn't believe she'd show it to Marsha, let alone hand it over to her. Why didn't Jackie just come to me? We could've talked about it. But share that with my worst enemy ever? I hoped Jackie knew what she was doing, because if Marsha had it, I wouldn't trust her. She'd probably give a copy to absolutely everyone.

I played the scene again. There I was, writing the e-mail. I clicked the little paper clip icon and the window rolled down so I could choose which document to attach. I clicked on Jackie White.doc.

Didn't I? I was sure I had.

But . . . wait.

Jackie White.doc?

Not *Jackie White Interview.doc?*

Was I stupid enough to save them with such close names?

"What an idiot!"

"Are you talking to someone else, Miss McMahon? Or are you generally this rude to teachers?"

"What? Uh, no, I uh, I didn't mean to—"

"Do you have something to add to the discussion?" Mr. Grudberg was standing in front of the chalkboard, hands on his hips, waiting for me to answer. When I didn't, he said, "Well, then, keep your jokes to yourself. We don't need any comics in this school."

He had no idea how much I agreed with him.

When I passed Ezra in the hall after class, he took one look at me and turned his back. He couldn't possibly know about the comic. Jackie would've done anything to keep it from him. Unless Marsha really did show it to everyone?

I decided that Marsha Pittel was evil enough to break into my house while I was sleeping, come into my room, open my computer, and . . . *get real, Addy.* She's bad, but she's not psychic. Psycho, maybe, but she would have no way of knowing about the comic. If Marsha *had* broken in and sent it to everyone, then I could blame her. But I was almost positive that was just wishful thinking.

Ez kept looking over his shoulder at me, giving me the evil eye.

Annoyed, I walked right up to him. "What?"

"What?" he repeated.

"Why'd you roll your eyes like that?"

"Why don't you do some investigative reporting and figure that out on your own," Ezra said, and hitched his backpack up on his shoulder. He turned to go.

"Wait!"

He stopped and brushed his bangs out of his eyes. I could see why Jackie might have a crush on him, but still. I said, "Just tell me. Please?"

He walked over, looking around to make sure no one saw him talking to me. "Nice job, Addy," he whispered. "The comic you did of me and Jackie."

"*No!* You saw it?"

"Yeah, I did. Why would you want us to read that?" Ezra said.

"I wouldn't! How—"

"Jackie forwarded it to us because she thought you sent her the interview by mistake. Everyone did."

"*Everyone* saw it?"

He continued, but not before squinting at me and shaking his head. "She thought you meant to send it to the Listserv. I guess she figured you'd written something nice. 'Cause you're uh, supposed to be *friends*?" He shook his head and his bangs flopped back down into their usual spot, over his eyes. "I gotta go."

So my whole day stunk like a skunk. Finally the last bell rang and I got out of there. More snow had fallen during school, and I skidded and slipped as I took the front stairs two at a time. I was watching my feet, trying to tell which patches of snow were covering ice and which were safe to step on. But since I have that gigantic curse on my head, *naturally*, as I made my way home, I spotted the worst two people I could possibly see.

Marsha and Jackie were walking a ways ahead of me, slipping and sliding even though they were holding on to each other for balance. I tried to go really slowly so they'd get to Jackie's house and go in, and I could sneak past to get home next door, un-noticed. I wasn't close enough to figure out what they were saying, but I could hear giggles and shrieks as they narrowly missed falling.

I had no one to hold on to though, so the patch they avoided was waiting for me, and I skidded and fell hard, right into a slushy puddle.

I got home, and after pulling off my cold, soggy clothes, changed into my favorite sweatpants and a clean top.

I opened the drawer that held the frame my dad made for me and reached for the old flannel shirt he used to wear. I kept it hidden so it wouldn't get washed. I buried my nose in it and I swear, I could almost still smell him. Finally, I couldn't put off calling Jackie anymore, and tucked the shirt away back next to the frame. I went down to the kitchen and picked up the phone.

"Hello?"

"Jackie?" I could hear whispering in the background. "It was an accident. It wasn't my fault!" I said.

"Yeah, well, Mrs. Metro assigned Ezra to work with someone else for lab, and I just know it's 'cause he told her anyone but me. So thanks a lot, Addy. He probably freaked out when he read *I wanted to marry him.* I guess that's not your fault either?"

"Well, I didn't mean for you to see that. Whoever showed that to you isn't a very good friend, you know."

"Good-bye, Addy," Jackie said, and hung up.

As I went upstairs, I could hear my mom and Jonathan laughing and talking. Empty cartons were stacked in the hallway.

"Well," my mom was saying as she wiped her hands off on a rag. "That's it. You're in. Now get to work!"

"Work? Have some mercy! I give up!" Jonathan said.

They were lying on the floor, looking up at the ceiling, laughing, when I walked in. I folded my arms and waited. Finally they noticed me standing there and tried to catch their breath.

"Oh, hi, honey," my mom said, leaning up on one elbow. She wore the grungy old art-making clothes she put on when she knew she was going to get messy. Her hair was under a bandana. Jonathan was just as dirty, in jeans and what used to be a white T-shirt.

"What were you doing?" I asked. "Playing leapfrog with the dust bunnies?"

They looked at each other and burst out laughing again.

"You—you—have a smudge right he-he-here!" my mom said as she tweaked Jonathan's nose with the dirty rag.

I sighed loudly.

Mom caught her breath and said, "Nicky is coming home from a playdate in about an hour, so we'll have dinner around six, okay? I'm making spaghetti and meatballs. Oh, wait. We had pasta for breakfast. All right, cornflakes it is!"

I gave them another super-huge sigh, which didn't do any good, and went to my room. The bugs Daddy and I had painted on my walls looked way too happy for my pit of misery.

I stared at my dark computer monitor. I didn't want to open my e-mail and check the *sent* folder. I didn't need confirmation of what happened. But it was like trying not to stare at someone with a big pus-y zit in the middle of their forehead.

It was so horrifying, you just had to look.

The computer booted up and I went to the e-mails I'd sent the day before. I clicked the attachment to open it. There it was. The reason I was now the most unpopular girl in the entire universe.

I *had* attached the wrong document. I was staring at "The Mental Adventures of Jackie White." *Ding!* I got the prompt that said I had mail. Someone was still e-mailing me?

No. It was from last night.

From: jackierainbow@mac.com
Subject: addy's interview of me
To: seelytimesstaff@mac.com

hi everyone-addy sent this 2 me by mistake and since im not supposed 2 see it im sending it out 2 u guys. Im trashing my file . . . its 2 tempting to have around!!!

jackie

I heard a door slam.

"Mom! I'm home!" Nicky called. "Addy! Mail's here and you got something!"

I trudged down the stairs and almost crashed into him at the bottom. Nicky wasn't watching where he was going because he had his nose stuck in his latest copy of *Weather or Not Journal*. He had this month's issue of *Chanticleer* wedged under his arm.

"Thanks," I said, as I slid it out from his armpit.

"Hope it doesn't stink too much!" he called after me.

I went into the kitchen and tossed my new *Chanticleer* onto the recycling chair.

I was done with writing.

I fiddled around with my sketchbook, but shoved it away and turned to my computer. I clicked the Get Mail icon and heard the depressing *bonk* that meant there was nothing new in my box. I just sat there, staring at the screen.

I was on vacation but it wasn't holiday-ish at all. Nothing was the same. I had waited in the dark on Christmas morning, but the sun rose, and for the first time ever, Jackie didn't sneak over for our secret stocking swap. She didn't come over in her pj's, her coat hiding the overstuffed, sagging, hand-knit stocking her mom made for her first Christmas. We didn't sit in my living room before everyone was up, like every year, dumping our stockings.

We didn't share all our little toys and gifts, and I didn't get to trade my candy canes for her chocolate. I'd sat there, alone in the quiet, thinking about the time a note fell out of her stocking.

We'd both gasped, thinking at first it was from Santa. Then we tried to muffle our giggles, because

Come home Now
or I'm opening
ALL your presents!
(even the ones
you didn't find!)

Love,
Mom

we were old
enough to know
who really filled
our stockings.

It hadn't felt
like Christmas,
because not only
was my dad miss-
ing, but this year
Jonathan was there,
and Jackie wasn't.

I shut down my computer and looked at the shelf over my desk, where Jackie's red-and-white-striped Christmas present practically screamed at me, "You have no friends!"

It was hard to believe it had only been a couple of weeks since the day Jackie chased me and I'd hidden it in my mother's room. So much had happened. I had forgotten all about stashing the package under the blankets on the chair in Mom's room, and in fact, no one knew it was there until Mom was getting ready to go to sleep one night and plopped down to the muffled crunch of a million broken candy canes. She was really mad because there were sticky red and white shards everywhere.

At least something good came of it. Nicky thought he scored when I gave him all the pieces. He didn't even care that they had all fallen out of the wrappers, that there were tiny bits of blanket fuzz on them, or that they were broken because of someone's butt. According to him, he'd hit the jackpot.

It was almost a week since Christmas, and I'd gone next door fourteen times to give Jackie her gift, thinking maybe she'd like it so much I'd be forgiven. But no one ever answered the bell. There is nothing more depressing than an unopened Christmas present six days after Christmas. Except maybe an unopened Christmas present with droopy green ribbons still tied to a million empty cellophane candy cane wrappers. The little red and white crumbs clinging to them somehow made it even worse. I couldn't take it anymore, and shoved it to the bottom of my backpack.

I went to my mom's room and dialed Jackie's number once again, but no one picked up. I was sure she was looking at the caller ID. How could I ever explain what happened if she wouldn't talk to me?

"Addy, come and get your last dinner of the year!" Jonathan called.

When I got to the table it wasn't set, but when I started to rummage through the fork drawer, Jonathan came in and motioned for me to stop.

He said, "I'm making dinner tonight."

My mom came into the kitchen and looked surprised. "You?"

"Yes, me. If you can eat macaroni and cheese for breakfasts, pancakes for din—"

"That was two weeks ago!" Mom interrupted. "And as I recall, you said you were just happy it wasn't cornflakes!"

"Well, how about last weekend when we had left-over pizza for breakfast?" Jonathan asked. He folded his arms and raised his chin in the air, like he'd won that round.

"You mean Nicky did, and that's only because he woke up so early I didn't have a chance to make him eggs or something, you know, appropriate."

Jonathan was looking behind her where Nicky was hopping back and forth from one foot to the other, using both hands to point in his direction. Jonathan cleared his throat and blinked a lot, trying to give him the international sign for Stop It or Your Mom Will Find Out What I Ate for Breakfast Last Weekend. His eyelids fluttered and snapped so much he looked like he was sending an SOS in Morse code.

Mom whipped around, saw Nicky doing his hoppy pointy dance, and then turned back to Jonathan. She burst out laughing. "*You* killed the pizza?"

Even though it was his fault Jonathan got busted, Nicky piped up, coming to his defense. "Jonathan didn't eat it *all*, Mom. He only had two slices."

Jonathan smiled. "I've been framed, I tell ya! But nevertheless, tonight *I'm* doing dinner."

The buttery smell that filled the kitchen made me think it might be something good, but when I saw the pot of melted butter on the stove, I asked, "Are we having artichokes? Because my brother won't eat artichokes."

Nicky wrinkled his nose. "Ew, yeah, I hate those things."

Then I saw that the big round coffee table in front of the TV was set. My mom saw it, too.

"Jonathan, you know I don't let the kids eat in front of the television."

Jonathan shushed her and shooed us out of the kitchen and into the den. "It's New Year's Eve, time for something special."

It reminded me that my friends—I mean, *ex*-friends—were probably doing something special. But I didn't even know what I was missing, because there hadn't been a single phone call for me, and it wasn't like my inbox was filling up with e-mail invitations no matter how many times I looked.

Jonathan asked us to sit on the floor around the table, and then brought out a huge platter of appetizers. There were mini hot dogs, tiny egg rolls, little bitty cheese puffs, and a bunch of other doll-size foods.

I had to admit, I was impressed. "You cooked all this?"

Jonathan laughed. "Only if pushing the button on the microwave counts. But they're delicious. My wife and I used to love appetizer dinners."

"You were married?" Nicky asked. "Did you get a divorce? Two different kids in my class are getting divorces now. I mean, their parents are."

Jonathan rubbed his forehead. He looked at Nicky,

then at the floor. "No. No divorce," he said quietly. "My wife died."

"My dad died."

He put his hands on Nicky's shoulders and leaned down so they were eye to eye. "It stinks, huh?" They nodded at each other. Jonathan said, "Anyway, this is the perfect dinner for family movie night."

"Cool!" Nicky yelled, and scooched in closer to the coffee table.

I didn't say anything. Even though I agreed it sounded like fun, and the food smelled great, Jonathan was staying in the *guest* room. That meant he was *not* family.

He picked up the remote, aimed it at the TV, and started the movie. Then he got a giant bowl of popcorn he'd made, poured the butter over it, shook some salt on top, and set it on the far side of the table. "For after you eat your hors d'oeuvres," he said.

We watched a really old movie called *Wonder Man* with this guy from the 1940s named Danny Kaye. It was pretty funny, and we laughed so hard I almost forgot I was cursed.

As we cleaned up, Nicky came running into the

kitchen. "Mom! Addy! Jonathan! Look, another snow-storm!" I went to the window next to the sink. It sure was snowing. Not just little light snow particles, but clusters of big, soft, floaty flakes.

I said, "When they're big like that, it never snows for very long."

"Uh-uh, Addy. And you are not the weather expert around here, anyway," Nicky said, still looking out the window.

Jonathan said, "That makes me want hot chocolate."

"Me, too!" Nicky agreed.

I told him, "Just because you read weather reports doesn't mean you're an expert either. It just means you're practicing your reading."

"I am, too, Addy. I *am* a weather expert." He glared at me.

"At least I'll get some writing done if I'm snowed in," Jonathan said. "I never seem to be able to just work all day long. I have to pay bills, or run errands . . . something always gets in my way."

"It's called stalling," I said, putting a platter in the dishwasher.

"Oh boy, are you right," he said, smiling at me.

I just nodded and stuck another glass on the top rack.

"Aren't you about due for your next interview?" he asked, and handed my mom a newly washed tray to dry.

I cleared my throat. "I'm done with that."

Mom said, "That's great, honey. I'm about done with my latest collage, too."

"I'm always relieved when I'm finished," Jonathan said.

I was finished all right. Finito. Kaput.

He added, "Congratulations, Addy."

"Why are you congratulating me on something you don't even think I do right?" I asked him. "I thought you were always telling me that my interview style was all wrong and I should do it your way?"

"I never said my way was better. It's different. There are lots of variations, and I just thought you might want to try other styles," Jonathan said.

I poured the detergent in the little soap cup thingy, swiveled the lid shut, and closed the dishwasher.

Nicky said, "Hey Addy, if this snowstorm keeps

going, maybe it'll bury the school and we'll never have to go back!"

"Yeah, until summer when it all melts, and we have to go then," I told him.

"Oh. If we had to miss summer vacation, I guess that would be part of the curse, huh?" Nicky asked.

"Addy," my mom said, turning to me, "what have you been filling his head with? You know there is no fairy curse. We've been over this. That's just one of Nana's stories. It's silly family lore—"

At that precise moment the steam valve on the radiator blew off like a rocket, hit the wall, and cracked the paint. It ricocheted and shot straight at Nicky's head, missed by one inch, and landed in his hot chocolate, spilling it everywhere.

"Sheesh clabeesh, Mom!" I yelled. "See? You were about to say something bad about the fairies, and look what happened!"

"Yeah," Nicky said, "You called the curse 'silly.'"

"That valve had been loose forever, you two. That's why it whistles. Well, whistled," Mom said, reaching for a dishtowel. To get to the spill, she moved the chair

119

where all the recycling paper awaited their final destination. "Honey, what's your new *Chanticleer* doing here? Take it upstairs, please. I don't want to dump it by mistake."

"Go ahead and recycle it. And you can cancel my subscription while you're at it," I told her.

She looked up from cleaning the chocolaty mess. "What are you talking about? That's your 'favorite magazine on the entire planet.'"

"Just never mind, Mom," I said, and headed upstairs.

I got my sketchbook from under my mattress. I used to keep it in my desk drawer where I stashed my dad's old shirt and the frame he'd made for me. I drew all the time, but I couldn't look at the frame that much.

I stared at the pad and slid out Dad's interview that was tucked between the pages for safekeeping. It was all handwritten, and in the margins he'd scribbled comments and arrows and stuff—his notes, giving me pointers. I cradled it in my hands, thumbing the edges that were too soft and worn to give anyone a paper cut.

If Daddy hadn't died, Jonathan wouldn't be in my

life. And if Jonathan hadn't been bugging me all the time to do interviews his way, or a *new* way, or whatever*, I wouldn't have been in such a rush to do Jackie's interview so I could get to my *Chanticleer* submission to prove to him I could write any way I wanted. It was complicated, but no matter how I figured it, it was all his fault. I wouldn't have confused one thing for another and messed everything up. And I wouldn't be the only person on the entire planet with no friends. I wouldn't have to give up writing.

But I did have to. I just couldn't chance anything ever getting mixed up again.

I looked at the interview in my hands. Maybe it could've won.

It might have.

I bet it would have.

I had worked on it for one year, ten months, and two weeks.

It only took a few seconds to tear it up.

"**Hey,** Addy?" I heard Jonathan's muffled voice through my door. Like I really wanted to talk to *him* right now. Maybe if I didn't answer he'd go away. I was lying on my back, looking at the dirty footprints on the wall next to my bulletin board. They looked as though they were walking up to the ceiling. Jackie and I made them last summer.

We had been lying on my bed then, too, our legs up with our feet braced. We started to notice how weird feet were, like something only an alien would have. Sometimes, when you say or look at a word over and over again it starts to sound like nonsense and it was kind of like that. My feet are perfect until you get to the end. Then they look bizarre. My baby toe is so much smaller than all my other toes, which are in a straight diagonal line, each a tiny bit shorter than the one before.

Jonathan was over that day, and he'd stuck his head in and scolded us when he saw what we'd done. That did it. We laughed for about ten hours after that.

125

I missed Jackie.

I stared at the footprints still walking toward the ceiling. I put my right foot over one and could see it had grown.

"I said, 'Can I come in'?" Jonathan was knocking harder now. I just kept quiet and stared at my almost perfect feet. Then—I couldn't believe it—the door opened.

"Are you kidding me? Did I say you could come in?" I asked, sitting up and folding my legs under me. I crossed my arms, too, and gave Jonathan my most annoyed look possible.

He stuck his hands in his pockets and leaned against the doorframe. "I knocked, and you wouldn't answer."

"What. Do. You. Want?"

"Hey, if you're having a hard time, I'm sorry, but don't take it out on me."

"Why not? It's all your fault." I lay down on my bed again and fit my feet back into their dirty shadows on my wall.

I could see Jonathan turning his head around and

cracking his neck. He always did that when he was irritated. "Addy, could you take your feet off the wall, please? Face me so we can talk?" *Crack crack crack* went his neck.

"I can hear you fine from here. And it's my room, and my walls, so do you mind?" I stayed right where I was.

"Fine, you can paint it yourself when it comes time."

"I'm never painting these walls. My dad and I did this together, and they're staying just the way they are. Forever."

He started to leave, but then he turned around, tucked his hands into his back pockets, and did his leaning thing again. "Why is your hard time my fault?"

I was going to tell him that if I hadn't been in such a rush to get Jackie's interview done in order to finish my dad's so I could submit it and win the *Chanticleer* contest just to prove to him I knew what I was doing then I never would have made the mistake of attaching the comic . . . sheesh, I was out of breath and I hadn't even said anything out loud yet. And that made me realize something.

". . . the mistake of attaching the comic . . ." echoed in my head. It would've been a great diabolical plan, but it was too complicated for even the evilest mastermind. Jonathan was a dweeb, but I doubted he was actually evil. It sure would be nice if I could figure out a way to blame Jonathan for sending that mean, rotten comic I made.

That *I* made.

If it were his fault, I'd be in the clear, but really, it was all on my own stupid shoulders.

I said, "Never mind. I take it back, okay?" I rolled over so he couldn't see my face. I swallowed hard, trying to force the lump in my throat to dissolve. I felt like I was being torn apart. Just like Daddy's interview.

Jonathan cleared his throat. "I only wanted to find out why you weren't interested in *Chanticleer* anymore. I thought you were all set to win the contest." When I didn't answer, he said, "We can talk about it another time," and shut the door.

My stuffed animals stared at me from their place next to my pillow.

"It was an accident!" I told them after Jonathan left.

They didn't say anything. Luckily. But they looked like they were thinking, *So what if it* was *an accident?*

I remembered something that happened with my dad a long time ago. We had this huge gigantic fight over his cigarettes. I'd completely crushed his last pack, and when he tried to grab them, he'd stepped on my bare foot with his work boots.

"I'm so sorry!" he'd said, hugging me.

"Why are you saying that if you're mad at me?" I asked.

He took my face in his hands. "I'm still angry, but I'm sorry I hurt you."

"But it was an accident."

"Even if something is a mistake, it doesn't mean you're off the hook for the apology. If you bumped into a stranger in an elevator, you wouldn't say 'It was an accident!' right? Saying 'I'm sorry' is hard. Your mom unstubborned me on that one."

I remember Mom piping in from the other room then, "Yeah, your dad would *never* apologize, and you're as stubborn as he is, Addy! One day, you, too, will see things my way—I mean, the right way!" They had both laughed then.

I looked at my stuffed animals.

She's your best friend? Rabbit Jones thought.

"Was."

You care about her? Mousey asked.

"Duh."

You made that comic. That was your choice. She saw it, and it hurt her feelings, right?

"Yeah, but..."

Go apologize!

I ran downstairs, got my coat, and went straight over to Jackie's to tell her how sorry I was.

If only it had been that easy.

BY THE TIME I GOT BACK TO MY ROOM, A MAROON MINIVAN WAS PARKED IN FRONT OF JACKIE'S.

MARSHA GOT OUT, RANG THE BELL, AND JACKIE ANSWERED **RIGHT AWAY**.

The next morning Jonathan and Nicky were already awake when I got downstairs. They were pawing through the basket Mom kept by the front door. Mittens, scarves, and snow pants littered the floor.

Nicky was saying, "I'm telling you, it was at least eight inches, and *I* predicted it!"

"You ought to be a weatherman when you grow up."

"A meteorologist, you mean," Nicky corrected.

They both looked up when I came in.

"Hey, Addy, I made a resolution last night. Guess what it was?" Nicky didn't wait for my answer. "Go sledding on the first day of the year! And I'm keeping my resolution, 'cause we're going to Killer Hill!"

"Nicky, a resolution isn't a prediction of what you want to do," I told him. "It's something you're promising to do. You're *resolving* to do it."

But he wasn't listening to me, too busy searching for something to keep his hands warm. He held up two mismatched mittens, considered them a moment, and stuffed them into the sleeves of his parka hanging on the hook next to him. He brushed past me and said, "Ahem, a blizzard, just like I predicted. No autographs, please."

I squinted out the window. Everything was so white, it looked blue. It seemed like someone had snapped a big blanket in the air and let it float down to settle on top of our whole neighborhood. It was like the world made a resolution to start a nice, clean new year. I wondered if I could start fresh today. Would it count if no one else knew?

After breakfast we all climbed into Mom's green VW bug. Our snow pants, parkas, mittens, and hats filled any extra air space that was left in the little car. I bet we looked like a stuffed olive.

Nicky stared out the window. "Even though it looks like the sun will poke through, we're going to get hit again." If he was right, maybe they wouldn't start school on time and I could avoid everyone awhile longer.

Jonathan pulled into the empty parking lot and said, "Last stop, Killer Hill. Everyone who wants to live a nice, quiet, boring life, stay in the car." He hauled himself out and said, "C'mon! Here, Addy, you take the red toboggan, and I'll use the flying saucer. Nicky and Cass, you guys grab the inner tubes. Race you to the top!"

Nicky actually started running and got as far as where the hill began to get steep. But they didn't call this Killer Hill for nothing. After five or six minutes, we got to the top, out of breath but ready for the ride to the bottom.

Jonathan sat on the flying saucer and dug his heels into the snow so he wouldn't take off before we were all ready. We got in a line and Nicky said, "Now this is what I call a race! On your mark, get—go!"

"Hey!" we all yelled, and went careening after Nicky down the hill. *Killer* Hill. Even Jonathan was screaming.

Huffing back up for the fifth time, Mom said, "I'm surprised no one else is here yet."

"You spoke too soon." Jonathan pointed to the parking lot, where three cars were unloading sledders. One was a maroon minivan.

"Mom, isn't it time we went back for lunch?" I did *not* want to see the people who were going to get out of that car.

"Honey, we've got plenty of time till then."

For the next four runs I was able to time it so I was going down while *they* were going in the opposite direction, and visa versa. But the next time I was dragging my sled up the hill it got away from me and I had to walk all the way to the bottom to get it.

"Hi, Jackie," I said as I passed her. I saw Marsha move her eyes back and forth from me to Jackie, which made her look even more weasly than she already did. Jackie just kept trudging up the slope.

Marsha said, "You *accidentally* let go of your sled? Gee, it seems like you're pretty good at *accidentally* making a *mistake* and letting things *accidentally* go and *hurt someone*, huh, Addy?"

The way she said my name made it sound like a curse word.

"And you know what? Jackie's the one who made a mistake by letting our friendship go, Marsha." It slipped out of my mouth before I could stop it. She had replaced me pretty easily as Jackie's best friend and I didn't want Marsha Pittel knowing anything I was feeling or thinking.

But I didn't need to worry. She had already turned her back on me and had caught up to Jackie.

My mom whizzed past and called out, "Meet me at the carrrr—"

"Aren't they coming?" I asked, gesturing toward Jonathan and Nicky, who were on their way back up the hill.

"I said I'd pack up their food and they could picnic in the car," Mom said.

"Oh. Well, is it okay if I stay home when you come back?" We leaned our sleds on a tree near the parking lot. I could feel her looking at me a second too long.

"What?" I asked.

Mom said, "Avoiding Jackie isn't going to make whatever you're fighting about go away, honey."

I stopped brushing the snow off my boots. "You *knew*? How'd you know?"

My mom gave me one of those smiles you must

learn how to do after you become a mother. She pulled me to her and I peeked out over her arm. No one was watching.

"Addy, the last time you've spent this much time apart from Jackie was before you ever met."

I relaxed into the puffy cushion of her jacket. That hug felt like a cocoon I didn't want to leave.

Until she said, "You can stay home after lunch, but I'm glad you came with us. It's a nice way to spend the morning as a family."

I broke from her arms and we got in the car. "Except for Jonathan," I said, "since he's not in our family. He's a guest."

"Well, for now, anyway."

"You mean he found an apartment?" This was great.

Mom gave me one of her looks and I thought she might get mad since I was so happy about him leaving. But she just pulled a tissue out of her sleeve and blew her nose.

"Ugh, I can't stop sniffling. Did you see Jonathan do that face-plant? He went headfirst into the pile of snow at the bottom!"

Mom kept talking and honking into her tissue, but all I could think about was how much better everything would be after Jonathan left. Then maybe we could get back to normal. At least, as normal as our family could be without Daddy.

I really didn't feel like starting the first day of the new semester by bumping into anyone, so I got to school as early as I could. I skulked down the hallways and kept my head lowered all morning until I thought my neck would stay bent like that forever. Since we'd had a snowstorm right before the break, I hadn't seen anyone from the day I became the most unpopular girl on the entire planet. I was positive everyone was watching me, thinking how horrible I was.

Even worse, during homeroom, I sat in the back of the class and when I went to take a book from my backpack, I found Jackie's crumpled Christmas present. I'd forgotten about it after shoving it in there. The wrapping was torn at the corners, and it seemed even more pathetic than before. I knew just how it felt. The candy cane crumbs had worked their way out of the torn cellophane and littered the bottom of my bag.

It took a lot of energy to avoid talking or looking at anyone. By the time lunch finally rolled around, I was starving. Then I almost lost my appetite.

There they stood, right in front of me, holding their lunch trays.

I don't know why I even bothered to say anything at all, considering how long it'd been since I'd had a conversation with Jackie, and Marsha just tortured me whenever I saw her. But I couldn't help myself.

"Hi, Jackie."

"What are you doing, Addy? Interviewing us for another comic?" Marsha spat. "We don't want to be your next subjects. Or should I say, *victims.*"

Jackie didn't say anything mean. But then, she didn't say anything nice, either. They sat down at the other end of the cafeteria and started talking and laughing.

I ate alone.

I pulled out my sketchpad and started drawing so I'd look like I had something important to do. I flipped back a few pages and continued working on the chapter in my autobiogra-strip about how my grandparents met.

On my way home from school, I saw Jackie walking

alone in front of me. No Marsha to be seen. After the way she'd acted at lunch, I was nervous about calling to her. We always used to go home together. Now I just walked behind her.

She went up her front walk and slipped a little, caught herself, and went inside.

I stood there, looking at her front door. Maybe if she didn't know it was me, she'd open it. Maybe Marsha didn't replace me. Maybe I should stop saying maybe and tell her I'm sorry.

"What do *you* want?" Jackie asked after she opened the door.

Maybe not.

"Never mind," I said. "This was stupid."

"No, I want to know. What do you want?" Jackie's hand gripped the doorjamb so hard the blood drained away from the knuckle bumps, like it was afraid to be there. Her right hand was squeezing something over and over. I finally realized it was one of those little soccer ball zipper pulls, like Marsha had on her backpack. She asked, "What am I to you, anyway? Drawing practice? Or actually, target practice?" She shook her head. "We had a pact, and you ignored it. You broke my trust and then on top of that, you made fun of me. I was humiliated in front of the entire *Times* staff!"

"Well, that part wasn't my fault," I said, my stubborn gene kicking in.

Jackie started to close the door in my face.

"Jackie, wait!"

"Yeah?"

"I'm really sorry."

"I'm really sorry? That's it? Gee, thanks so much, Addy. Bye."

That's when I stuck out my shoe so she couldn't close the door. It seemed like a good idea at the time. But my foot got slammed.

"Ow!"

Jackie looked at me like I had just told her a pink fairy in some kind of flying space orb had confirmed the family curse. "*I'm really sorry,*" she said, and slammed the door shut.

I hopped on one foot, holding the other, and sniveled like an idiot. This was horrible. And *not* at all how I imagined the apology going. I hobbled down the front walk and just as I was hoping she wasn't watching me out the window and thinking I was a big giant loser, I stepped on a patch of ice and shrieked as my legs flew straight up in the air. My body spun like a top, and I landed in a huge pile of snow.

I sat there, rocking back and forth, trying to nurse my left knee and my right foot at the same time.

The front door opened, and Jackie stood there, hysterical. I couldn't believe it. I went over to apologize, and she ended up laughing in my face!

Carefully, she made her way over to where I was sitting, probably to rub it in. I stared at her, frowning. My embarrassment was way worse than the pain in my knee *and* my foot put together.

I started to say, "I really don't think—" but at the same time, Jackie's foot met the patch of ice that attacked me, and *her* legs spun out of control, and she went down on *her* butt.

Without looking my way, she slowly turned around to get on all fours. But since she wasn't wearing mittens, she had no traction and her hands slipped, and she fell flat.

I pressed my lips together, but the smile went into my cheeks, and I snorted. I hid my face with my hands, and started coughing, hoping to cover my giggle.

I heard a sob, and peeked through my mittens to see her shoulders shaking. She was crying so hard she wasn't making any sound. I turned away and rolled onto my knees to try to get up.

"Aaaaaaahhhhhh!" I heard her wail. I winced, and turned to look. But Jackie wasn't crying. She was laughing. Laughing so hard she was starting to wheeze.

I smiled. Then giggled, and after that I couldn't stop, and the two of us laughed our heads off.

When she could breathe again, she gasped, "Are you okay?"

"Yeah. Now I am. You?"

We sat there together in the snow, warm from laughing, until I said, "I'm sorry, Jackie. I mean, really, really sorry. No way did I want to hurt you. I'll never write ever again, I swear."

148

Jackie had a leftover smile from the laughing, but her voice was serious. "It's the stuff you made up that got me so upset, Addy. I just couldn't believe you'd do that, and then *send* it to me to read."

"That was an accident!"

"Yeah, right."

"It was so stupid of me." I took a deep breath and tried to tell her everything as fast as possible, before she could stop listening. "All you could talk about was Ezra. And then you started saying that stuff about my mom and Jonathan getting married and even though it's totally not true, I got mad. After I did the comic, I wasn't even angry anymore. No one was ever supposed to see it. I just did it for myself. I named it 'Jackiewhite.doc.' I called the real interview 'Jackiewhiteinterview.doc' without even realizing how close they were, since by the time I finished the interview, I'd forgotten all about the comic. Everything got mixed up and you never should've seen that, because I only did it to make myself feel better, not for you to feel bad, and, well, it's all my fault and I'm sorry."

I got up and Jackie did, too, and we both stood there not knowing what would happen next.

Jackie hugged her sweater tighter. "I didn't want to kiss Ezra, you know. That made it even worse. Well, that and you made me sound completely self-involved and boy crazy. I was just wondering what I'd do if he tried to kiss me. I was *worried* about it, not *hoping* for it. You're my best friend, and you didn't even know the difference. I thought you were so cold, putting all that stuff in and then expecting me to read it."

"You're the one who's cold," I told her, and gave her a little nudge.

Her teeth were chattering. "Yeah, I'm freezing. Do . . . you want to come in?" She didn't wait for me to answer, and walked gingerly back to her front door.

I stepped over the nasty patch of ice and followed her inside. "Wait a second. I just thought of something. Why have you been hanging with Marsha if she gave you the comic to read? That's not a very nice thing to do. I mean, *making* the comic was bad, but I didn't *mean* for you to see it."

Jackie's face got very red then and she stared at the carpet. "First, of all, Marsha did not show me anything." She looked up at me, but her cheeks glowed brighter, and her eyes went back to the floor. She said, "I was mad at you for one other thing."

I gasped, afraid I was in trouble again now that we had finally made up.

She heard and looked me in the eye. "I was angry that you tried to tempt me."

"You knew I sent it to you on purpose?" Now I was really going to get it. Even though I was standing inside her house, I was sure I was going to be shoved out the door and straight toward that ice slick.

"Duh, Addy. What, you thought you were being so sneaky, sending it to me?"

"But," I protested, "I wrote the message to the group!"

Jackie looked at me with one of her how-long-have-we-known-each-other? looks. She said, "I was so mad at you for trying to trick me into reading the interview, tempting me that way, but I was good, and forwarded it to everyone. Later that night I couldn't resist anymore and went into my trash folder, fished it out, and opened it. *Then* I was mad at you for sending that comic. *Then* I was mad at myself for falling into your trap."

My mouth dropped open, I was so surprised. "*You* opened it and read it yourself? I thought you'd been so noble, and had resisted. I'm so, so, so, so sorry, Jackie, I—" but she didn't let me finish.

"No, Addy, I was doubly angry, but I should have been only, um, singly angry. So, I guess what I'm trying to say is, um, I'm sorry, too. If I hadn't opened it, I probably wouldn't have seen the comic. If I learn anything from this, maybe next year I won't even peek at my Christmas presents."

That reminded me. I reached into my backpack and pulled out her gift, battered as it was. I said, "I know this doesn't look as pretty as it used to. It had a rough holiday." I started to hand it to her, but stopped. "Wait a second. You didn't want to kiss Ez?"

We smiled, and for no reason at all, we ended up collapsing in giggles on the floor.

"I-I-I have to—to—to tell you s-s-something,"

Jackie gasped between gulps of laughter.

"Wha-what?" I asked. She stood and started up to her room where we always had our most private conversations, and I followed. After we scooched up onto her loft bed, I was ready to hear what the big secret was.

"I know why Ez didn't want to be my lab partner," Jackie started.

"I'm sorry. I know it was because of me." When she didn't continue I tapped her foot. "Right?"

Jackie picked little balls of fuzz off the blanket and made a tiny pile, like she was harvesting them for the next cold night or something.

"Um, no. I think"—four more fuzz balls met their doom—"he was scared that I liked him 'cause he liked me, too, and knowing I liked him made his liking me more of a real thing, like, we couldn't admit it before, but if it's out there, and we both knew about it, well."

"I understand *completely*." I had *no* idea what she was talking about. But maybe Ez did like her.

"Only guess what? Mrs. Metro asked if I would

tutor him because he's not so great at science, and I am. So now we're meeting twice a week. Cool, huh?" Jackie smiled at me, looked at the package still in my hands, then back at me, this time wiggling her eyebrows. She was quiet for a second, but because she *is* Jackie, blurted, "When do I get to open that smushed-up package?"

I almost forgot I was still holding her present. "I'm glad you saw it when it looked pretty," I said, handing it over.

"Wow, Addy!" she said after ripping off the already torn candy cane paper. "This is the best drawing you've ever done in the history of doing drawings!" She jumped off the bunk and placed the portrait I'd done of the two of us right next to her championship soccer trophy. She climbed back up and thanked me. "I don't have anything for you, though. I was too mad."

"Oh. Oh, well. I guess I should just be happy you forgave me," I said.

I think it was obvious I wished she'd gotten me a present, too, because then Jackie looked around her bed and grabbed the mushy pillow I always played with when I came over. It had slinky green fabric and was filled with tiny balls of plastic or something. She tossed it in my lap and smiled.

"Don't ask me to wrap it, too," she said. I grinned back at her and squished the pillow around.

It was quiet and I picked a couple of fuzz balls myself. "Jonathan found an apartment and is going to move out," I said.

Jackie gave my shoulder a little shove. "Get OUT!"

I pushed her back and said, "Stay IN!"

"So you were totally right and I was completely wrong," she told me, spreading her hands out and shrugging.

I thought about my mom's bare ring finger, and how she looked when she said she and Jonathan were falling in love. Even though the room was warm, my whole body shivered.

"I don't know if you were completely wrong, but at least he's leaving. Maybe he'll finally stop talking to me about how to write."

"Wait a second," Jackie said. "What did you tell me before about never writing again? Why did you say that?"

"Because if I give it up, no one will ever get hurt again."

"So you're not doing your autobio . . . autobiographic . . . strip . . . thingy anymore?"

"That's not real writing. That's just comics; it's mostly art. I never want to confuse anything again, so I've given up writing interviews."

"You are so demented! Of course the comics count as writing, and anyway, wasn't it the comics that got you into trouble, so why quit doing your interviews? And also, what about the *Times*?"

"Huh? What do you mean?" I asked.

Jackie sighed one of her famous exasperated sighs and said, "Addy, obviously I don't want any more mix-ups, but it was what you wrote *about*, not the format you wrote them *in. Doy.*"

She flicked my shoulder. "Besides, you love doing your interviews. You're famous for them now and you'll disappoint all your readers. Plus, you're going to win the *Chanticleer* contest with your dad's interview."

"It can't win."

"It totally could," Jackie insisted.

But I knew it couldn't because it was gone. Torn, tossed, and at the bottom of the town dump. Where it belonged.

When Jackie was mad at me, every day felt ten years long. Since we made up, it seemed like it'd only been a week, even though more than a month had whizzed by.

The one thing that stopped the clock was *The Seely Times* staff meeting. Every Wednesday was the absolute worst day of the week for me, now that I wasn't doing interviews anymore. I was amazed at how much I missed talking to all those important people like local celebrities and politicians. I had to admit, being the interview queen was very cool. Everybody knew who I was because of it. The town paper even did a feature on *me* on what life's like for a kid reporter.

I had told Jackie to let the staff know I quit the paper. Even though I wasn't surprised no one was begging me to come back, I kind of wished they would. Today there was a teacher conference and since we were dismissed before lunch, the weekly meeting was canceled. It was a nice break from my usual Wednesday misery.

But no matter how hard it was, I couldn't give in. I had stopped writing as my New Year's resolution, even though I knew from experience that keeping one of those things wasn't easy. My dad always tried to quit smoking on January 1. The only time he succeeded was the year he died. He joked, "I guess it's true. Cancer really does cure smoking!" I didn't think it was funny, but like I said, he had a weird sense of humor.

I was in my room, making a list of all the people I wouldn't meet because I was never going to do another interview, when I heard a knock. I yelled, "Come in!" at the same time the door opened.

"Mom! You're supposed to wait till I say 'Come in'!"

"You did say it."

"Yeah, but not before you opened the door," I pointed out.

"Sorry, honey. I'll do better next time, but this is heavy," she said, flipping the laundry out of the blue plastic basket, raining a huge pile of pants, shirts, and socks onto my bed. They were still toasty from the dryer.

I turned myself around to lie on them.

My mom curled her hair behind her ear. Which reminded me she had no ring on, which reminded me about what I'd told Jackie the day we made up.

"Mom?"

"Uh, huh . . ." She started folding my favorite pair of jeans, but instead, held them up by the belt loops. "Do these still fit you?" They did a little dance in the air as she jiggled them around, waiting for my answer.

"Yes," I said, and grabbed them from her. "I can fold my own laundry, you know."

"I realize that, but you never do," my mom said, smiling. "And I don't want you adding to my laundry mountain by mixing your cleans and dirties."

"When Jonathan moves out, you'll have less. When's that happening, anyway?"

"I don't know."

"He *is* going to move out, though, right? I mean, we talked about this way back on New Year's Day, coming home from sledding."

"Why do you think he's moving out?"

"Because," I said, "you told me he wasn't going to stay in the guest room forever. It's practically spring now, so when's that happening?"

"It's February, and I don't know."

"What do you mean, you don't know? He's *not* staying in the guest room forever, right?"

My mother sat down next to me, and stroked my hair. She took the tip of my braid and painted my face with it, the way she used to when I was little. It tickled across my forehead, down my nose, above my lips, and in circles around both cheeks.

"*Right*, Mom?"

"I hope not," she said, dropping my braid and getting back to the laundry.

I knew it. My mother was on *my* side. She didn't want him living here forever either.

"Addy, why don't you want your *Chanticleer* subscription anymore?"

"I just don't."

"It seemed kind of sudden," she said, smoothing the wrinkles from a shirt folded over her arm.

How could I explain that reading *Chanticleer* was

too painful, because just *seeing* the magazine reminded me of all the stupid mistakes I'd made. It forced me to remember that I would never write again, or look forward to being a professional writer when I grew up. I had hurt my best friend, thrown away my dad's interview, and lost my dream of being a published writer. If I started telling her why I couldn't read it anymore, it would start a big talk about Jonathan, and my interviews, and even more stuff I didn't want to get into.

"I'm just over it, okay, Mom?"

"All right," she said, standing. She picked up the empty basket and started to leave. "How long has *that* been there?"

I followed her horrified gaze and looked at the shelf over my computer. My latest Plate of Appeasement offering had sort of melted into a g-ross mush. I was probably better off never trying to appease the fairies: at least then it wouldn't seem like I was attempting murder by food poisoning.

My mom made a face as she took the pile of toxic waste and held it as far away from herself as she could. "Oh, and honey, we need to go dress shopping soon."

"What for?"

"The Platinum Pencil awards are formal, and you don't own anything fancy enough."

I groaned. "Do I have to? Besides, it's not for a million years."

My mom took a deep breath. "It's next month, and yes, you have to."

"Why?"

"Because it's a big honor that Jonathan won, and we're going." Before she closed the door she said, "And Addy, I don't want to hear any more complaining about this."

"But Mom—"

"You will go to this dinner. You will behave properly, or you will be very grounded."

Totally depressing. But I knew one thing that would cheer me up.

"Hey, you want to hang out?" I asked Jackie when she answered the phone. "Since we had an early day, I already got my homework done."

"Well, that depends. I'm getting together with Marsha, Ez, and Leon and I can tell you've been avoiding them since, you know, the Thing," Jackie said.

Since we were past it, we hardly ever mentioned the comic/interview mix-up, but when we did it was the Thing. I did not consider spending time with Marsha Pittel a good way to get cheered up, and I could tell that's where Jackie was headed. Ever since we had made up, she'd been trying to get Marsha and me to be friends. We'd been putting up with each other for Jackie's sake, but that was as far as it was going.

"Ad? You still there?"

"Yeah, I'm here."

"Okay, so anyway," Jackie continued, "I know you've been avoiding those guys and we're meeting. Just the lead staffers."

"A *Times* meeting? But school's out for the afternoon," I said. Uch, another Wednesday that would take a million years to pass. I wondered if I could get hypnotized so I wouldn't miss being on the paper.

"I know, but Mrs. Crimi said the building's open, and other after-school stuff is going on, so we could come in since we had so much work to do before the next issue. She said she'd poke her head in when she could."

"Okay, well, never mind then. Have fun at your meeting," I said, totally *not* cheered up.

Jackie cleared her throat, which she always does when she's either angry, or nervous about telling me something. Or when she had a cold, which I knew wasn't now. "Addy?" she said.

"Am I about to get yelled at?" I asked.

"What? No, I have to tell you something," she said. This didn't sound good. "I kind of didn't tell anyone that you quit the paper."

"Why not?" I said louder than I meant to. So that's why no one was begging me to come back; they didn't know I was ever off the paper.

"Because," Jackie explained, "I was hoping you'd change your mind. Your interviews are so good. Don't stop just because of a stupid mistake."

I said, "I can't risk it, Jack, and now everyone will

think I spaced on all those meetings or something. This is going to make me look even worse!"

"Look," Jackie said, "I told them you were slaving away on my interview, trying to make up for what happened. They needed time to get past the Thing anyway. Why don't you just come to this meeting with me? You must miss writing, right?"

It seemed important to Jackie. I didn't have to agree to start writing again. I could keep my resolution. I'd just go to the meeting, see what was what. And it was the least I could do to try and get along with Marsha. For Jackie's sake.

"Fine. I'll be there."

"Good. See ya. Why don't you come over and we'll walk together?"

I ran downstairs and practically crashed into Jonathan as I rounded the bottom of the banister.

"Whoa!" Jonathan yelled as he reared back and sloshed coffee all over his shirt.

"Tell my mom I'll be with Jackie, okay?" I said, pulling on my coat.

Jonathan was walking up the stairs, the wet shirt

pinched between his thumb and finger, tenting the coffee stain away from his body.

"Tell her yourself. I have to change my clothes."

"You're going upstairs anyway," I pointed out. I opened the door, but stood there with one hand on the knob, because now Jonathan had decided to come back downstairs.

He still held the front of his shirt. The empty mug was in his other hand, and he pointed it at me.

"Do you honestly think I'm in the mood to do you any favors after you just caused me to pour hot coffee all over myself?"

I looked outside and could see Jackie waiting. I stuck my head out and yelled to get her attention, and gave her one of those I'll-be-there-in-a-second gestures. I closed the door and turned to Jonathan. "It's not like it's a big favor, and besides, that wasn't even my fault. It was an accident."

Jonathan said, "What has that got to do with anything? You could still be courteous and apologize."

"Fine. I'm *sorry* you spilled coffee all over yourself." I opened the door again. Before I walked out, I said,

"Now will you please tell my mom I went to the school with Jackie?"

The little bump in his temple was pulsing in time with his jaw, and he cracked his neck. "Yes. I will tell her. But you're going to have to work on your manners if we have any chance of getting along," Jonathan said, turning around to start back up the stairs again.

I was going to ask him why would I ever want a chance of *that*, but Jackie was hopping around now and waving her arms for me to hurry up.

I walked out the door and stuck my mittens in my pockets. It was pretty warm out for February and I barely needed to zip up. Even though there were puddles where snow had melted, they were topped with a thin layer of ice, like they couldn't decide whether to freeze or not. Bubbles of air had gotten caught under the icy surface, and I crunched along, crushing them under my feet.

While we walked, Jackie filled me in on everything that was going into the next issue. I didn't have the heart to tell her that I was just tagging

171

along for the day. We were on the front steps of the school when the minivan pulled up. The door opened and Marsha, Ez, and Leon piled out and ran toward us.

Jackie yelled, "Hi, you guys!"

"Hi, Jackie," Marsha said.

"Hey, Jack," Ezra said, smiling and blushing from under his blond fringe. Jackie smiled back. I said nothing and no one said anything to me.

As we all walked toward the stairwell to go up to our headquarters, Leon and Ezra lagged behind, arguing over which they should do, a new art column or a regular feature on practical jokes.

"Of course the pranks would be more popular," Marsha said, turning around. "Until someone actually did one and got in trouble."

Then Marsha and Jackie looked at each other and said, "Art column" at the same time. The boys sulked until they got to the room and saw the snacks Marsha had brought. "For *after* we get some work done." She dumped them on the table and everyone took a stool.

They went over all the usual *Times* business. Nobody seemed to notice I wasn't contributing any comments. As I listened, I felt myself relax, and it was kind of like after I rub lotion on my dry skin in the winter. I stopped feeling all itchy, and everything was comfortable again.

Jackie cleared her throat and gave me a look that said, *Give this a chance.* "Marsha, Addy's saying she's going to quit writing, and I think we need to do something about that."

"What? Congratulate her?" Marsha asked. I didn't say anything, but I did try to send evil fairy curse vibes straight at her head.

"Marsha, you have to admit, everyone loves her interviews," Jackie said, glancing over at me. "We need to convince her to keep doing them."

Leon said, "I'm taking this art class with Ez, and there's a kid from that private school across town. His cousin goes here, and he gave him our first issue. The kid told me when he lent it to someone, he never got it back because it made the rounds."

"Oh yeah," Ezra said, "That was a great issue.

Everyone wanted to read the interview you did with the police chief."

Leon stood up and pounded his chest with his right fist. "Because why? Because he loved to, how'd he put it? 'Make mischief'!"

Marsha snorted, and told him to sit down and forget about the practical joke column.

Jackie looked at Ez. "*You* take art class?"

Ezra looked hurt. "I can't draw, is that what you're saying?"

"No," Jackie said, "I just never knew you were interested."

"There are a lot of things I'm interested in that you don't know about," Ez said, brushing his bangs aside. Jackie blushed.

I knew Ezra was handing me a peace offering by telling me about that kid, and I appreciated it. But I just couldn't go back to interviewing. Then nothing would get messed up again.

Leon jumped back up and started pacing. "Hey, Addy, why don't you talk to that kid in eighth grade who's going to the National Spelling Bee? We could have a sidebar of all the words he's won with so far and do a quiz or something."

Jackie stood up and got her notebook. She leaned against the table facing us, and started scribbling. "That's a great idea, Leon. We could add a definition list at the back and—"

"Hey, maybe we could do a contest!" Ezra interrupted.

"Yeah, that's a good idea, too." Jackie put her notebook down and looked at me. "What do you say, Ad? Will you do it?"

It sounded like it could be a really great interview, and I found myself composing the opening paragraph. I could start with something like "How do you spell s-u-c-c-e-s-s?" I'd have to ask Mrs. Crimi if that was a cliché already.

All of a sudden I realized something. It was really the writing I missed, not meeting all the cool people, or how everyone knew I was that girl who did the interviews. I was always thinking about words and the exact right way to put them together to grab the reader so they'd feel something. Like a punch to the heart. Little descriptions popped into my head all the time; how it felt to wake up, or the way someone walked, or whatever. Even though I hadn't been putting anything down on paper, my mind couldn't stop that easy.

It would be tempting to do just one more. Just this spelling champ kid. But what if I made another mistake? What if someone got hurt again?

I couldn't risk it. No friend should ever have to suffer from what I wrote.

"Hey," Marsha said, "if Addy doesn't want to do interviews anymore, don't push her."

She was on my side? Was this an alternate universe or what?

Marsha continued, "I could take over the interviews, you know. I'd do them a little differently, of course, but we could still have stories on interesting people."

That was the last straw. Did Marsha want everything that belonged to me? First kickball, then soccer, after that, my best friend, and now doing interviews? I couldn't stand it anymore. "What is it with you?

Are you trying to take over my entire life? Would you like to sleep in my room, too? Wear my clothes? No, I know. You wish you could change your name to McMahon, because who'd like a last name that reminds people of a *toilet*?"

Before Marsha could say anything, Jackie smacked the table hard and said, "That is *it*. You two are impossible! Can't you at least *try* to get along?" When neither of us answered, she folded her arms and said, "Okay, you know what this means. We're playing Truth or Dare." We all groaned at the same time, and Marsha gave me a dirty look.

"No, seriously," Jackie said, "sharing the truth can open up friendships, and if you're both going to be my friend, you'd better start now."

We thought we were saved when the door opened and Mrs. Crimi came in. She was carrying a big thermos and a stack of white Styrofoam cups. "Hard at work, I see? This hot apple cider was left over from our conference. I'll try to come back later and look over what you've done." She set the thermos and cups down in the middle of our table and waved good-bye as she closed the door behind her.

Marsha said, "Oh, we forgot about the snacks I brought." We all sat back down at the table and munched on a nutritious balance of Jujubes, potato chips, and dried mango. Leon opened the Thermos, and I could see the vapor curling up and disappearing. He poured a cup for everyone, and I took a slow sip. The cinnamon-y steam tickled my nose.

Jackie said, "Look, I'll go first." We all groaned again.

"Okay, but remember, it was your idea!" Leon said. He slumped over the table, leaned on his elbows, tapped his fingertips together like he was some kind of evil genius, and asked, "Since the sixth graders are having a dance, if someone asked you to go to it, who would you want it to be?"

I don't think Jackie expected that question because she turned the exact same color as the bottle of Pepto-Bismol my mom keeps in the medicine cabinet. "Uh, I uh, I don't know," she stammered.

Ezra warned in a singsong voice, "You hafta answer or you get a dare."

178

"So you're saying you want a dare?" Leon asked too quickly, and jabbed Ez with his elbow. No one would ever want a Leon Ravets dare, if they knew what was good for them. He was famous for his practical jokes, which was why he wanted to do that column.

I smiled, and so did Marsha, and accidentally we looked at each other. And stopped smiling.

"Okay, fine," Jackie said, sitting up straight. "I'd want Ezra to ask me."

Marsha and I giggled and looked at each other. This time we didn't stop. But that didn't mean we were friends or anything.

Leon smacked Ez and said, "So, now's your chance, sucker!"

Ezra shoved Leon off and wiped the potato chip salt from his hands onto his jeans. He combed his fingers through his hair and rubbed his eyes. He cleared his throat, took a deep breath, looked over at Jackie, and finally said, "Okay, so . . . you wanna go?"

"Sure," Jackie said, and smiled.

Marsha said really fast, "Nextquestionmyturn."

179

Leon and I swiveled toward her, but Ezra and Jackie kept looking at each other out of the corners of their eyes, smiling little smiles, like they had a secret, even though we all knew what it was.

"This one's for you, Addy," Marsha said, folding her arms across her chest. What could she possibly want to know about me?

"Are you the one who got everyone to completely ignore the *proper* pronunciation of my name?"

I gave her my most innocent look possible. She was horrible, but she wasn't stupid.

"You *know* what I'm talking about," she said.

Yeah, I did. It started right after Marsha moved in and took over my spot as best kickball player in the entire grade. After this one game, when my team had gotten totally massacred, all the kids ran to the drinking fountain. There was a big line. I was fifth from the front. I saw Marsha go to take a drink. She was so happy about the kickball game, and I was so mad. Since she was new, she didn't know about the tricky button and how you had to push it a certain way or you'd get a bath. Marsha pressed the little

180

silver disk, and instead of arcing up, the water squirted out straight and got her right in the crotch of her pants. When she turned around, some kids giggled and said it looked like Marsha had an accident. They were laughing about it when I whispered, "I guess that's why she's called Marsha *Piddle!*" All the kids laughed like crazy. And it stuck, no matter how many times she said, "It's Pit-*tel*! Like French!"

Now everyone was looking at me. Waiting for my answer.

"It wasn't my fault," I started, but Marsha stood up so fast she practically knocked her stool over.

"I *knew* it! I *knew* you were the one! It's not *piddle*! It's Pit-*tel*! Like French! Do you know how many years I've had to live with that horrible nickname?"

"Marsha, your pants were wet and the kids were already laughing about it. I, uh, I didn't mean to—"

Marsha's voice hit a note only dogs could hear. "There are *still* people who call me that, and every summer I hope it'll be forgotten, but some boys never do, and when I walk down the hall, they tease

181

me. They whisper gross things in class, and if I turn around, I have no idea who's saying it. I have to make sure the coast is clear just to go to the girl's room because you wouldn't believe what a simple visit to the lavatory can do to start up the worst of those idiots!"

Leon and Ezra had slumped over the table, building towers of Jujubes and flicking them over. Jackie cleared her throat and stared into her cup, swirling the cider around, moving her hand in slow circles. Marsha sat down again and covered her head with her arms.

"I, uh, I gotta go," I mumbled, and disappeared out the door.

Since I had so much practice when the Thing happened, I was great at avoiding everyone I knew on the entire planet when I was at school the next day. Until lunchtime.

I felt a tug on my jacket just as I was getting to the cafeteria. For a second I thought maybe it was Marsha and I was about to get my butt kicked like a championship soccer ball. I turned, but it was Jackie.

"Addy," she said, pulling me out of the line by my sleeve.

I was scared to find out what she was going to say after all we'd been through. If everyone hated me again, maybe I could get my mom to move to a different town? We could get rid of Jonathan at the same time. Very convenient. I really couldn't take her being mad at me again. I had the urge to cover my ears and yell, "La, la, la!"

But Jackie started talking anyway. "Did you get the math homework from—"

"You're talking to me?" I was *so* shocked. And *so* happy.

"Of course I am. Why wouldn't I be?" She looked completely confused. Then she realized what I was thinking. "Because when you were like, nine, you basically called someone a pee-pee head? Please."

I laughed and gave her a big hug.

"I'm not mad, but after you left, Marsha told us that when she moved here there was only one thing she wanted. It wasn't a backyard to play in, or a room of her own, or even a friend. All she was hoping for was that no one would notice her stupid last name."

"Wow."

"Yeah," Jackie agreed. "Leon tried to make her laugh about it, but I guess it's hard to have a sense of humor about a name that makes you such a target."

"What'd he say?"

"He told her some jokes and stuff, but that didn't work. Then he just suggested that she get married young, but to make sure the guy's name was Smith."

"Jackie! Let's go!"

We both looked up to see Ezra at the top of the stairs looking annoyed. But still really cute.

I saw Jackie blush. She turned to me and smiled like crazy. "Gotta go do some tutoring!" She started up the steps, but held one finger at Ezra, and ran back down to where I was still standing, trying to decide whether to hit the lunch line or not. Sometimes going in late was worse than skipping lunch and being hungry, since only the g-rossest choices were left.

"Addy, you do realize at some point you're going to have to apologize to Marsha, right?" Jackie asked. I could tell she didn't actually want a conversation about this right now, because even though she was looking in my direction, her whole body was pointed up the stairs.

"It's not like it's my fault everyone glommed onto that nickname," I said.

"You are the stubbornest person I know, have I ever mentioned that?" Jackie asked, slowly creeping back up the stairs to where Ezra was waiting. "What about all that 'oh, my dad taught me how you're supposed to say I'm sorry when you do stuff, even if—'"

"—it's an accident," we both said.

Ezra was now bouncing around on the balls of his feet. He was not very good at hiding his impatience. I looked at Jackie and said, "Just go. Come over later and we'll talk some more."

I looked for Marsha to say I was sorry, but okay, I admit it, I didn't look *that* hard. We had been super archenemies for a long time. It wasn't so easy to just forget about that. But by the time I got home, finished my homework, and was sitting around reading one of my old comics, I was considering maybe it was time to get over this whole feud thing. Later.

The comic was one of my favorites, about my parents falling in love. It showed my dad in high school, putting one of his little animal carvings in Mom's locker. He used to hide them for her, like secret messages. I'd drawn a cow carving but now I thought it looked kind of like a hippo. I glanced at my computer when I heard it bong. It was Jackie, IM-ing me.

Jackierainbow: sup?

Writergurl: how r u?

Jackierainbow: Gr8. deciding wht 2 wear 2 the dance. u?

Writergurl: i forgot 2 tell u – i cant go!

Jackierainbow: no way

Writergurl: way.

Jackierainbow: y not?

Writergurl: the pukey pencil awards

Jackierainbow: lol but stinko!

Writergurl: 8-(

cant believe dork-o jonathan gets a writing prz

and i hve 2 sit thru the stupid ceremony!!!!!! its going 2 b sooooooo boring!!!!!!!

Jackierainbow: HEY! deadlines coming!!!!!!!

Writergurl: ??

Jackierainbow: doy addy! chanticleer?! did u send in yr dads interview?

Writergurl: remem. im done writing? got rid of evrthing.

Jackierainbow: u hve 2 do a nu story.

Writergurl: nw. got in 2 much troubl b4.

Jackierainbow: i told u – it was wht u wrote – not THAT u wrote. dont quit writing.

I heard my mom calling me to the phone. Then she hollered, "Dinner's in ten!"

Writergurl: g2g. l8r –

I picked up the phone in my mom's room. "Hello?"

"So are you quitting, or submitting?" Jackie asked without bothering with "hello." "I mean, if the

187

interview with your dad is anything like the comic you made of me, you totally could win, Addy."

"Are you kidding me?"

Jackie said, "Well, now that I'm not mad at you anymore, I do have to admit it *was* kind of funny—in a mean sort of way—but still, Addy, pretty good. Is that what your autobio-strip is like?"

"Autobiogra-strip. Yeah," I said.

"Why haven't you ever shown them to anyone?"

"Sheesh clabeesh, Jack, we've been over this a million times," I said. She didn't get it. Why would I ever show anyone? It was full of my secret thoughts, like any personal journal. I tried again to make her understand. "It's supposed to be private, Jack. Like your diary. Would you share that with anyone?

Jackie said, "But I didn't know how cool it was. I mean, that comic was more than your private thoughts. It was great because you had the drawings, like in your interviews, plus it had more, I don't know. You, like, made a story out of it."

Once again I felt like I was in an alternate universe. "You are crazy, you know that? I hurt you so bad, and now you're saying how great it was. Do you have any idea how freakishly weird that is?"

Jackie laughed. "I know, but I'm just looking at it more like an editor. It told a story."

"Kids! Dinner's in thirty seconds!" I heard my mom yell.

"I gotta go, Jackie."

"Addy, just think about this one idea I had, okay?"

"What?"

She said, "How about sending in a comic for the *Chanticleer* contest?"

"*What?*"

"Send in your autobiogra-strip. Ha! I said it!"

"No way! Like I want my entire private life on national display? International, if you count Canada. It'd be totally embarrassing."

Jackie sighed the way only she can. "Don't answer, just think about it. If you did a new one about your dad, maybe it could help other kids who have the same situation. It wouldn't be like you were baring your naked soul."

"Ew, Jackie."

"You know what I mean. Other kids would see they're not the only ones who go through stuff like that. Anyway, it's just an idea."

I got downstairs to find my brother watching The Weather Channel.

"How's it going, Nicky?" I plopped down on the sofa next to him in time to see someone's house fly away. "Yikes. What're you watching? Aren't there any cartoons on?"

"It's *Tornado Time*. But the forecast is coming up in a sec," he said, not taking his eyes off the TV. "I thought we were going to get a big spring snow-storm, but I was wrong. We had a pressure sys—oh, wait—it's starting." Nicky turned up the volume. I didn't hear anything the weatherman predicted, though, because the only words in my head were Jackie's.

Every time I thought of my autobiogra-strip on display for everyone to judge, my stomach felt like I'd jumped off a cliff. It's true I've wanted to win the *Chanticleer* contest since I started writing inter-views . . . no, since I started writing, period. And, I admit, I've dreamed for a long time about seeing my name in a real publication. But send my private journal out there for the world to see? Even if I did one just for the contest . . . it's so personal. I couldn't imagine anything good about this idea, and I doubted there were a lot of kids who went through what I had, anyway, no matter what Jackie said.

The morning whizzed by, which was surprising for a Friday. Jackie and I had a "meet and eat" planned. She wanted to try to talk me into doing a new comic for *Chanticleer*. It was going to take a lot of convincing, though.

I'd brought a sandwich, so I avoided the line and stood at the front of the cafeteria. It smelled like a mix of school spaghetti, ranch dressing, and soggy snow boots. Not what you want to be sniffing when you're about to have lunch. Between the odor and the fact that all the tables were full, I almost decided to skip eating, but I had to wait for Jackie. Then I saw her talking to Ezra at the far left end of the cafeteria. They were wedged into a packed table, facing away from me.

I started to head over there and almost walked right into Marsha exiting the lunch line with her tray.

Before I realized who it was, I said, "Oh! Sorry!" I almost saw steam coming out of her ears. It was one of those automatic "sorrys," one of the easy kinds.

You say it to strangers you might bump into in an elevator, and it made me think of Jackie, and how much it would mean to her if I gave Marsha a real apology. But it did have to be real. From the heart, real. Jackie was always forgiving me for something, it seemed. When I said I was sorry, she accepted it, and we moved on.

Marsha was looking for a seat in the overcrowded room. She'd always been so nasty to me, but now that I thought about it, maybe it was because she always suspected it was my fault everyone messed with her name.

Of course she'd hate me. She gets something good happening like beating the best kickball player in the whole grade, and what happens but she gets completely humiliated. It must be horrible to be branded with a name that sounds like baby bathroom talk. It really was time to end this feud.

I had plenty of things to be mad at Marsha for, but—

Wait, didn't I?

What had she ever *really* done to me? I thought back to when it all started, in fourth grade. I had gotten angry because she was better than me at kick-ball. Okay, she creamed me in *two* sports: kickball and then soccer. But so what? If I had cared that much, why did I quit? I could've stayed on the team and gotten more practice.

I started doing my interviews then, and it turned out I was better at writing than I was at soccer. And I liked it more. I didn't *really* have plenty of things to be mad at Marsha for, but I did have a lot of other bad stuff going on that year. The day our teacher introduced her to the class, I ran home and told Daddy about the new girl. And he told me about his cancer.

I looked at Marsha now, working hard at ignoring me while she still looked for a spot to sit.

"Can we talk?" I asked her.

"No."

"Please, Marsha?"

"Fine. Go ahead," she said, still scanning the room for a place to eat.

I looked around and saw, all the way in the back, one empty table.

"C'mon, we can sit over there."

"I'm not *sitting* with you," Marsha said. "Just say whatever you have to say."

I grabbed her arm and pulled her toward the far end of the cafeteria. "Jackie wants us to talk. I'm going to try because I at least owe her that."

She couldn't pull away or her entire lunch would splatter all over the floor. I dragged her through the maze of tables until we got to the back of the room.

"Have a seat," I said.

"Just talk and get it over with," Marsha said. She wouldn't even face the table and stood with her back to it, holding her tray.

"I am really sorry, Marsha. I hadn't even thought about how hard it must've been all this time. Really. I couldn't figure out why you hated me so much."

It didn't seem like she was listening, and I wanted to make sure she really *heard* me.

"Marsha, I need you to sit down now, okay?" I tugged on her sleeve. It must've gotten her off balance because both arms went up, still holding the tray, and she clocked me in the mouth with her

198

elbow. We both thumped down on the bench at the same time.

No one was at this table because an entire can of . . . *something* . . . had spilled on the bench. It was sticky, liquidy, and pale yellow, and we were sitting right in it.

"*You did this on purpose, Addy McMahon!*" Marsha's eyes filled with tears. "How sneaky can you get?"

"I didn't! I swear! I didn't know!"

"You are so mean. You set this whole thing up. And now my pants are wet and I have to walk by every guy who has ever laughed at me. *Everyone* here will see, and *ohhhh . . .*"

"I swear, Marsha, I didn't do this on purpose. I wanted to apologize for ever messing with your name. I should've warned you about the drinking fountain, but I was so mad you beat me in kickball, and started getting picked first all the time, and my dad was sick, and I was mad, and it was the only thing I was good at and I just wanted to—to—" I tried to get everything in at once.

Marsha kept her head down; the untouched lunch

sat in her lap. A tear fell onto her sandwich and rolled off the cellophane wrapper.

Our bottoms were completely soaked by now. We were still just sitting there, neither of us wanting to move. Getting up would mean complete humiliation. And we were in the back of the cafeteria, so we'd have to walk past every single kid there.

Then I realized the worst thing ever. I was wearing *white pants*. Maybe I could stay here and just be late for my next class? But I'd still be wearing the pants. For a second I considered sneaking home to change, but that would never work—too many obstacles. What if I went to the girl's room upstairs—there was one of those hot air hand driers in there. But the thought of sticking my butt under that thing wasn't so appealing either—someone might come in and then everyone would tease me for *that* too.

Then I remembered something great! I had my sweater with me! I could tie it around my waist and no one would ever see a thing.

"I can't believe this!" Marsha cried.

"I—"

"Shhh!" Marsha interrupted. "Never. Speak. To. Me. Again." She twisted around and dumped her lunch onto the table. Slowly she stood, looking around to see who was watching. She held the empty tray behind her, over her rear, but she might as well have pointed a giant neon sign right at her butt.

I knew what I had to do. There was no choice. I grabbed my sweater from around my shoulders and before Marsha could take another step, lassoed her around the waist with it, tying it there. It would've been more graceful if I didn't have to untangle her hand still holding the cardboard tray under the sweater, but I figured it was the thought that counted.

I said, "I owed you one."

She looked at me, tightened the knot, and sniffled. Then she turned and walked away through the cafeteria, no one noticing a thing.

But now it was my turn. I stood up. Everyone seemed to be involved in their little lunchroom cliques. I walked toward the front of the cafeteria as though nothing were wrong.

But then, through some kind of kid humiliation radar, one student, then another, then another, noticed the enormous, wet, pale yellow stain as I passed. Pretty soon everyone in the cafeteria was laughing and pointing at me. At my *rear end*. It was the most embarrassing moment of my entire life.

I was about halfway out when I saw Jackie and Ezra in the crowd of kids. Ez was trying not to laugh, and Jackie was wide-eyed, her hand covering her mouth. She tried to give me a sympathy signal, but then I saw Marsha. She was probably enjoying my mortifying moment. I was not going to be able to get out of this with even a crust of dignity, I could tell. But at least it was just one moment. What if every day were made up of situations like this? All at once, I knew that was what it must be like for Marsha, with that name of hers.

She walked right up to me, and I was ready for whatever I deserved. There we stood, eye to eye, my face beet red and my behind pee yellow. I waited.

Marsha put her arm around me and covered my butt with her empty lunch try. For good measure, she turned around and stuck out her tongue at my abusers.

From then on we were known as "the Piddle Sisters."

My mother tried to take me to Lovely Ladies Evening Wear the minute I got home from school. Then she saw my wrecked pants. "What on earth did you sit in? And why are you wearing your summer pants, Addy?" She shook her head at me. "Go put on something clean, and then we'll go dress shopping. Hurry up, though, who knows how long this will take."

I booted up my computer while I was changing. I wasn't sure if Jackie knew all the details about me and Marsha. I didn't know if we'd be friends now, but at least we weren't enemies anymore.

Bong!

You have been invited to a group chat by Jackierainbow and Run2Fast.
Accept or Block access?

I wasn't sure who Run2Fast was, but I knew who ran too fast and guessed it was Marsha.

Writergurl: Hey.

Run2Fast: j. told me u quit writing & tht is not kewl (& i told her abt wht u did)-

8-)

Writergurl: am i in alt. universe or is marsha im-ing me?!

Jackierainbow: LOL-i told her abt the contest

Run2Fast: ya & dont kill me 4 saying this, jackie - the comic was actually prtty good – art was kewl. if the story wasnt mean it wldve been gr8.

Writergurl: i AM in alt. universe!!!!

Jackierainbow: i won't kill u b/c i already told her tht! seeeeee addy?!!!

Writergurl: g2g buy a dress for the putrid pencil awards. jack - fill marsha in abt jonathan etc etc OK?

Jackierainbow: L8r

Run2Fast: L8r

Writergurl: L8r

We got to Lovely Ladies Evening Wear, which was right next door to Lovely Ladies Lingerie Shoppe. You could get your fancy schmancy dress and then go over and get underwear to match. Pretty soon you'd be able to get a complete makeover when the Lovely Ladies Salon opened. The owner liked to say (and don't forget the sweep of the arm), "They call me magical Madame Jeannie, because like a genie, I can always make your wish come true!" She knew most of the women in town from years of bra shopping.

It was hokey, but I didn't mind, especially since the potentially never-ending dress hunt could end right there at Lovely Ladies.

Mom led the way, and I trudged behind. I was distracted, though, thinking about Jackie's idea. But there was no way. It was ridiculous. I could never let anyone, let alone the entire universe, see my comics. I made a mental list of all my reasons.

#1—Everyone would know my private feelings.

#2—What if I lost the contest?

#3—What about my resolution to never write again?

#4—But comics didn't count as real writing . . . did they?

Madame Jeannie found me daydreaming in the back, herded me toward the changing room, and hung a pale blue dress on the hook. I stepped through the curtains, and they closed behind me like water after a dive. I looked in the mirror. An okay-looking girl with no smile looked back at me.

"You are never going to get published," I told my reflection.

"Don't you want to win the contest?" it asked me.

"Not worth it," I said.

I struggled to reach the zipper in back and finally got it up after contorting myself into some kind of circus performer position. The dress had long sleeves and fit snugly around my ribs and waist. It flared out at the skirt part. I swiveled around so it swung back and forth, making a satisfying swishing sound. Every time I swirled the skirt, dust angels flew across the beam of light spilling through the high dressing room window. My dad would've loved this dress.

"So, do you, Addy?" my mom was asking.

"Do I what?"

"Do you like it? Would you be comfortable wearing that dress? Can I see it?" My mother poked her head in and gave a little gasp. "Oh, honey. You look gorgeous. You could wear the pearls Nana gave me when I married Daddy. They'd look great with that dress. The pale blue, with white pearls? Just stunning."

"Yeah, Mom, this is okay." I took the dress off, got back in my regular clothes, and put my jacket on.

As we drove home, Mom was all excited, saying things like "Those pearls will be perfect" and stuff like that.

I watched the trees rush by. They were still bare, but spring was definitely on its way. And so was the *Chanticleer* deadline.

On Sunday morning, the scent of cooking bacon filled the house, waking me up and boinging me out of bed faster than a trampoline catapult. Someone should make a bacon alarm clock that spritzed that smell right up your nose. It would sell like crazy. My stomach made a sound like a lovesick sea lion.

Everyone was already eating by the time I got to the kitchen. On the menu were huge, gigantic bacon, lettuce, and tomato sandwiches.

"Smells great, Mom," I said. "Is there one for me?"

"Morning, Addy," Jonathan said, biting into his sandwich. Tomato glop squished out the back and oozed down his fingers. He looked like he was starting to enjoy our weird menus.

Nicky was holding his with two hands, mayonnaise gushing out between the layers. He took a bite and said through a mouthful, "Hey, Addy, guess what? I watched the news and the weatherman said there was going to be an early spring, but I was tracking the storm on a site I found and I bet you anything, he's wrong! I'm going to e-mail the station and ask for a job as a junior meteorologist. Isn't that a great idea?"

"Definitely," I said.

He beamed at me. "You mean about my career?"

Something about my nine-year-old brother using the word *career*, cracked me up, and Jonathan, too, and we both started laughing.

Mom smiled. "I think a great idea would be for

you to finish chewing before you share your life plan, if you don't mind."

I took the empty seat next to Nicky. I lifted the white paper napkin covering a lump on my plate and found my sandwich, waiting for me, still toasty. I *love* BLTs. The warm B, combined with the cold mayo and crunchy L, plus the juicy T. Yum city.

"Honey," my mom said, wiping a bit of mayo from her lip. No one can stay clean eating these monsters.

"Mmmm?" I answered, my mouth full. I took a swig of juice and said, "Yeah, Mom?"

She got up to get more OJ. "Tell Jonathan about the dress you got."

Jonathan looked at me, waiting for the big report.

"Oh, well. It's nice," I told him.

"Um, good," he said.

"It's a gorgeous dress and Addy looks stunning in it," Mom said.

I was thinking, *That doesn't mean I'm going to have a gorgeous time in it,* but my mouth was too busy eating to start a fight.

I cleared my place and ran upstairs to brush my

teeth so I could go next door. Jackie, Marsha, and I were hanging out for the day.

"So, did you send it?" Jackie asked when I got to her house.

"No. I told you, it's private."

Marsha said, "I didn't realize your stubbornness stretched into your writing, even." When I looked at her and there was a silence, she added, "That wasn't a dig, I'm just saying."

Jackie said, "You *are* stubborn! You still have time. The deadline's not for seventeen days."

"It would be so cool to see your name on their site, even if you lost. Which you wouldn't," Marsha said.

"Well," I told them, "I wouldn't want to lose, that's for sure."

"You'd never even have to worry about that," Marsha assured me.

"Nope," Jackie added, "you wouldn't."

"Forget it, you guys."

But ten days later I was on the *Chanticleer* Web site, staring at the big, red counter that ticked off the hours, minutes, and seconds until the deadline. I *really* wasn't that interested in the contest, but the flashing, spinning, and ticking gizmo thingy hypnotized me.

And then my screen went black.

"Mom!" I hollered as I ran downstairs. "My computer just crashed! Can I use yours?"

"It's on the table. You can use it while I run out for a bit if you promise to stop yelling," my mother said, grabbing her keys. "Jonathan's working upstairs in his room—"

"You mean his boffice?" Nicky called from the den.

My mom shook her head. "Just let Jonathan know I'm doing errands if he starts looking for me, okay?"

She left and I opened her laptop, returning to the *Chanticleer* site. I wondered what it would feel like to log on and see your title listed as the winner. My stomach flipped just thinking about it.

I grabbed a glass of juice from the fridge and took a sip as I clicked on a link called Previous Winners' Circle. As it opened I heard *bleep*!

I read the entire page, but couldn't tell what kept

making the sound. I collapsed the window and as soon as it closed, I realized what was bleeping. Someone was sending me an instant message.

Moviefreak: I said, R U there?

Who was MovieFreak and why was she IM-ing me? Maybe it was a pop-up from the *Chanticleer* site? I typed in "YES." As soon as I did, I felt like an idiot, because the screen said:

Gardengirl: YES.

MovieFreak was IM-ing my mom, duh, not me. It bleeped again, and before I could tell her I wasn't who she thought I was, she replied.

Moviefreak: I know we've been over this, but as long as we don't tell the kids about our engagement, they're going to think of me as just a guest. You know how much I love you? I want to be a family!

I gasped. It wasn't a *she* messaging my mom. It was a *he*, and I was pretty sure I knew which *he* it was. I stared at the screen, not knowing what to do.

Bleep!

Moviefreak: My editor just called – I've got to work – C U L8R!

I quit the program, slammed the laptop shut, and ran out the front door.

Jackie was right!

I would never win the *Chanticleer* contest. I wasn't going to be published. And to top it all off, my mom was going to marry Jonathan.

I *was* cursed.

I'd been crying on Jackie's bed all afternoon.

"It's okay. It'll be okay," she kept saying. She patted my back while I sobbed into my hands.

"How—how—how could this be ha-ha-happening?" I wailed. "Why couldn't everything just stay the same? Why does she have to *ma-ma-marry* him?"

The phone rang somewhere in the house, we heard footsteps, and then Jackie's mom knocked on the door and opened it a crack. "Addy? Your mother wants you home for dinner."

Jackie peeked down from her loft bed where we'd been huddled, and asked, "Is it all right if Addy has dinner here and then sleeps over?"

"As long as you'll both eat leftovers, and it's okay with her mother." She walked back down the hall and we could hear her talking into the phone. Finally we heard the clickety click of her shoes coming back. "Addy?" Jackie's mother said. "Your mom's okay with you staying, but you'll need to be home tomorrow no later than two o'clock sharp because a reporter from the paper will be over to interview the family and take pictures."

"What for?" Jackie asked.

Mrs. White said, "Something about Jonathan's award."

After she left, Jackie and I stayed in her room until it was time to eat. Later, we ended up watching a movie. I was all talked out, anyway, but Jackie knew it was a big help just to hang out together.

We woke up late and decided to walk down to the diner and get something to eat. We called Ez, Leon, and Marsha to meet us.

"I'm positive I'll go down in history as the unluckiest person on the entire planet. This curse will last forever, and I will live a life of misery," I told them once we were settled in a booth.

Leon asked, "What curse?"

Ezra groaned, and Jackie clucked her tongue. She said, "Don't get her started."

The waitress set Marsha's food down. She picked up a fry and held it like a mini corn on the cob, eating the crusty edges off first before covering it in ketchup and stuffing it in her mouth.

My food hadn't come yet. "Can I have one?" I asked, reaching for her plate. I could smell the mix of hot, deep-fried potatoes and vinegary-sweet ketchup, and my mouth watered watching Marsha's munch and drench routine.

She swatted my hand away. "Yours is probably in the fryer at this very moment. Be patient." She picked up another golden fry and waved it in front of my nose. "Oohhh, these are soooo good."

I was too fast for her, though, and snatched it away, popping it in my mouth before she could protest. Ez and Leon cracked up.

Jackie said, "Addy, there is no such thing as a real curse."

"Oh yeah?" I said. "First my dad dies. Then I drew that stupid comic and mixed it up with my interview file. Since I gave up writing, I'll never have another chance to win the *Chanticleer* contest, and now my mom is going to marry Mr. Dweeb?"

Leon leaned closer to Jackie and said, "Please tell me that's not his real name."

Marsha laughed and said, "Now *that* would be worse than Pittel!"

I said, "Don't you mean—"

Ez, Leon, and Jackie chimed in, "Pit-*tel*, like French!" They all cracked up, including Marsha.

Leon clapped her on the back and said, "*Now* you're getting a sense of humor!"

Without missing a beat, Marsha looked at Leon and deadpanned, "Don't touch me," and they all collapsed again.

"As I was saying," I said, trying to refocus everyone, "if all those things aren't proof of a curse, or at least, the most horrible luck in the entire universe, what else would you call it?"

My order arrived, and Leon said, "At least your food isn't cursed. Looks good. Can I have some?"

I smacked his hand away, just like Marsha did mine a second before. He pretended to nurse his entire arm while I dug into my fries. I took pity and tossed him a couple.

Ezra said, "Sometimes life just stinks, Addy."

"Yeah," Jackie said, "that's what I always tell her."

"And sometimes you make the bad things happen," Marsha said. She quickly added, "That wasn't a dig. I mean, everyone makes mistakes, and the stuff that happens because of it makes it feel like bad luck, but it's just what happens after you mess up."

Leon said, "My mom calls it 'the consequences of your actions young man.' Only for you it'd be 'young woman.' No, 'young lady,' right?"

Ez elbowed him.

"Well, maybe some stuff just is what it is, but let's not forget his stupid award dinner is the same night as the dance, so I miss out on that, too," I said. "And, today at two, I have to get all dressed up and take some stupid pictures so he can be Mr. Famous in the paper."

"Addy? That's like, soon," Ezra said.

"Oh no! What time is it, exactly?"

Jackie looked at the clock on the diner wall and said, "Don't worry, it's only one thirty. We can get the check and walk home in plenty of time."

The waitress was delivering food to the next table. She said, "Hon, don't you go believin' that clock.

That thing's slower than the cook during the lunch rush."

"Do you know what time it really is?"

She put the rest of the food down and hunted around her apron pocket. Pulling her watch out, she said, "Darlin', it's about two fifteen or so."

"Doesn't matter if I'm cursed or not now, because I am so dead."

I tried to run all the way home, but those fries were like a bag of bricks in my stomach and I got a cramp.

Mom was sitting on the sofa, where she could watch the front door. Next to her sat Jonathan. They were all dressed up, but my mom hadn't even put her makeup on yet, so maybe I wasn't in trouble after all.

I was wrong.

But I thought I was right, because the first thing she did was jump up and hug me, hard. As soon as she saw I was all in one piece, that's when the yelling started.

"You were to be home by two o'clock sharp, young lady!"

Leon sure was right about that "young lady" stuff.

"How could you do this? I told you to be here. We had to call the reporter and push back the appointment. Do you think you're the only one in the family?"

Nicky stood in the doorway, plugging his ears with his fingers.

"*Family?* Jonathan isn't *in* our family. Oh, wait. I forgot. Yeah, I am the only one in the family . . . the only one who didn't know you guys were getting married!"

Mom said, "How did you know about that?"

"*Moviefreak* told me." I crossed my arms and stared at Jonathan.

His eyebrows jumped up and his eyes practically fell out of his head. "That was *you* I was IM-ing?"

My mom and her *fiancé* exchanged a look.

Nicky took his fingers out of his ears and said, "You're getting married?" He went to Jonathan and looked up at him. "Wait. You're going to be, like, my dad?"

227

"Nicky," I said, pulling him away, closer to me, "no one is *like* our dad, and Jonathan isn't even close." I turned to my mom. "You lied to me. You said he wasn't going to live in the guest room forever. You're a liar!"

"Addy!" Jonathan gasped. "I can understand your being rude to me, but I won't allow you to talk to your mother like that."

"You can't tell me what to do! You are not *my father!"* Before he could say another word, I ran up to my room just as the reporter rang the doorbell.

I lay on my bed, crying my eyes out for the second day in a row. When Daddy got sick, I couldn't do anything about it. And now Jonathan was going to ruin our family, and there was nothing I could do about that either.

Unless . . .

I went over the reasons I hadn't wanted to enter my autobiogra-strip.

#1—Everyone would know my private feelings.
#2—What if I lost the contest?

#3—What about my resolution to never write again?

#4—But comics didn't count as real writing . . . did they?

But, if I did decide to submit it,

#5—Jonathan would see that he wasn't welcome in our family.

#6—Possibly forcing him to get out while he could.

I looked at the calendar. I had less than a week until the deadline. So what if the whole world knew my private thoughts? If it would get Jonathan out of my life, it would be worth it.

I got to work right away. I'd need to rewrite some of the comics to have the strongest possible impact on a reader who didn't know me. It had to be more . . . what was that word Mrs. Crimi always used . . . more *global*.

I had no idea how long I'd been at work when I

heard my mom say, "Addy?" She came in and sat on the bed next to the desk, where I was sketching.

"I know. I have to get dressed for the stupid reporter."

"No, she left. You needed to cool down, and I didn't want your anger at me to ruin Jonathan's interview." She took a deep breath and ran her fingers through her hair a few times, trying to figure out what to say. Finally she spoke. "I'm sorry I didn't tell you about the engagement. I didn't mean to lie to you, but I never said he was moving out of the house."

I stopped drawing and looked at her. Was she kidding? I shook my head and looked away.

"Okay, maybe you have a point," she continued. "But when you asked me if he'd live in the guest room forever, I said 'I hope not' because I was dreaming of the day we would live together as husband and wife."

"How could you not tell me?"

"I didn't think you were ready, honey. I know this has seemed fast to you—"

"It doesn't *feel* fast to me; it *was* fast. It's only

been one year and eleven and a half months since Daddy died."

Mom held up her hand to stop me from interrupting again. "The grief counselor told me that if you've had a good marriage, you're more likely to find yourself in another good relationship that much sooner. Anyway, Addy, I was hoping you'd start to like him if he were around a lot. Or, at least, not hate him."

"He's not my father," I told her.

"Of course not, honey. No one will ever replace your dad. But Jonathan can be a man in your life without being your dad."

I shook my head. "I don't *need* a man in my life, Mom. That's the whole point."

And to prove it, I stopped talking to Jonathan.

Over the next five days, I felt the *Chanticleer* deadline hanging over me, like homework I knew I'd never finish. I didn't have time to do a whole new comic, which I think would've been a better idea, but I reworked what I had. It told the story about my dad getting cancer, and how Jonathan horned in on our family, and what that felt like. I had to cut a lot, because even though my word count was under the contest rule limit, I knew they wouldn't be able to print an extra-chunky-size edition just because my autobiogra-strip had more pages than the average story.

Two nights before the deadline, I was printing everything out, and of course, since I'm probably still cursed, I ran out of ink. I e-mailed Jackie to see if she had any spare cartridges.

The phone rang almost immediately. "Got your post," she said when I picked up. "What're you working on?" She had a smile in her voice, and I could imagine the smirk on her face. Jackie knew me so well.

"I just ran out of ink." I twirled the phone cord around my finger.

"I knew it! You *are* submitting something! C'mon over. I have two color and one black."

When I got to her room, Jackie tossed me a bag with the ink.

"Thanks," I said. "Lucky we have the same printer. When I win, it'll be because you had this!"

"No problem," Jackie said. "Wait—have you broken your vow of silence yet?"

"Nope."

"How long do you think you can last?" she asked.

"Well," I said, counting on my fingers, "I only have to wait until my entry gets published, since when he reads it, he'll leave so fast we'll have to ship his stuff to him."

"Addy, *what* are you sending in? I thought you were doing something about losing your dad?"

"You'll see when it hits the newsstands," I told her.

Jackie said, "Anyway, I'm glad you're submitting

something. And I'm glad you decided to break your New Year's resolution and start writing your interviews again."

"Yeah, it feels good to be back. Lucky Marsha convinced me to talk to the spelling champ."

"Marsha! I thought *I* was the one who told you to keep writing!" Jackie exclaimed.

"Okay, okay. Sheesh clabeesh, you'd think you'd be happy we were friends now," I said, smiling.

Jackie threw a pillow at me as I left her room, and I headed back home to finish printing out my entry.

The next morning I went into my closet and knelt down on the floor. I reached toward the very back, where I kept the little plastic cash register I'd had since I was six. I pushed the button and the drawer popped open, making the coins inside bounce out onto the carpet. I counted as I gathered them, adding the total to the dollars I'd stuffed into the bill slots. There was just enough to send my submission overnight. Tomorrow was the deadline.

I walked down to the post office and slid the stack of paper I'd printed the night before into the express mailer envelope, sealed it, and pressed down on the flap for good measure. I drew a picture of myself on the front, pointing to the address. I kissed it, and gave it to the clerk.

Then I crossed my fingers.

Why can't time go quickly when you're waiting for something important? Every day felt like a week in the dentist's chair, while taking a math test, while recovering from a bad case of poison ivy in the spot between your shoulders where you couldn't reach. And to make it even worse, I had to go to the Painful Pencil dinner, so I wouldn't be able to check the *Chanticleer* Web site every ten seconds, like I'd been doing in the weeks since the deadline.

Ignoring Jonathan was pretty easy for me. I never had to ask him for money, since I got allowance from my mom. I didn't need homework help, so what else was there? I had to admit, mealtimes were the hardest because I couldn't ask him to pass me anything. But if I wanted the salt at dinner and it was next to him, I just went without. Sometimes you have to suffer when you are fighting for your beliefs.

But for the most part it was even kind of fun, puzzling out ways to get around talking to him. Usually it went something like it did last weekend when I went into the Closet to ask my mother for a ride. Jonathan was there, watching her work.

"Mom, can you take me to Marsha's?"

She said, "I can't, I've got to finish this collage before the layers dry. In a couple of hours I might be able to tear myself away."

Jonathan said, "I can drive you, Addy."

"Okay, Mom, thanks anyway," I had said. "I'll see if her mother can pick me up."

By last week I could tell he was starting to get really annoyed; he was cracking his neck a whole lot more than he used to. Maybe when he read my *Chanticleer* entry, it would push him over the edge and he'd run from the house, screaming.

"Addy." I heard over the loud knocking on my

door. "I'd like to talk to you," Jonathan said. I had no idea how he was going to do that, since *I* didn't want to talk to *him*. I guess he couldn't take it anymore because when I didn't answer, he called, "If you don't open up, be forewarned: I'm coming in."

I sat at my desk with my back to the door, but I heard it open, and a few seconds later, the sound of Jonathan's neck cracking confirmed that I was stressing him out.

"Can we please stop this ridiculousness, Addy?" I didn't turn around, or say anything, so he just kept talking. "I either get the silent treatment, or I hear you speaking rudely about me when I'm standing right there. I don't deserve that kind of disrespect. I've been nothing but nice to you. So we didn't tell you we were planning on marrying. We needed to make sure you and Nicky were ready."

I turned around. It couldn't be helped, because this was too good to resist answering. "Well, I'm not ready. I guess you'll call off the wedding, now, huh?"

"I'm sick of your behavior."

"So leave," I said, turning my back on him again.

"Look," he said, "it was our news to share when we thought it was the best time." He cracked his neck again. "What have I done that's horrible enough to make you hate me so much?"

I couldn't think of any one thing. I just kept seeing what was left of our little family, being ruined by *him*.

"You're supposed to be a *guest*! You know what my dad always said about guests? They stink like fish. Until they leave. Or something like that. Can't you just leave already?"

Jonathan stood there, blocking my doorway like a giant boulder. He said, "Hey, you're stuck with me, so you might as well get used to it."

It seemed like I was lost in a maze and had nowhere to turn. Every direction led to a dead end; I felt claustrophobic. I couldn't take a deep enough breath. My stomach burned, and it made me think of a show I'd watched with Nicky about volcanoes. The weeks of silence built up and bubbled inside me like hot lava, and all of a sudden, I couldn't keep it in anymore. I exploded.

"I don't *want* to get used to it! It isn't fair! Why can't the clocks just run backward? I want my dad!"

I heard someone screaming and realized it was me. I hadn't meant to even *talk* to Jonathan. The last time I screamed like this was at my dad because he wouldn't quit smoking, to stay alive for *me*. That was before he found out he had cancer. I had always thought of his sickness like that: little *c* cancer, not the big *C* kind. That's what *other* people got. The ones who died. *He* wouldn't die. He'd beat it.

Jonathan didn't ruin our family. The cancer did that.

I looked up. Jonathan was still standing in the same spot, but something had changed. He didn't look like a boulder anymore. He seemed softer; his shoulders slumped, and he'd stopped rubbing his neck.

I hadn't even realized I was crying. I covered my face with my hands.

"It's okay, Addy. It's okay," he was saying, as he came over to pat my back. "I'm so sorry. I'm such an idiot. I've handled this all wrong. Of course you want your dad. Of course you do.

"Shhh. Shhh. I know. I remember what it's like. After my wife died, I was angry at the world. And here I've barged into your life, and your home, and only thought about how happy we could all be. I guess it's because I haven't been close to anyone since my wife died, and when I met your mom all that changed." He handed me a tissue, and I blew my nose. "You know, I was so happy when I found out you were a writer, too. I thought we could have something in common."

I blew my nose again and said, "Funny way to show it."

"What do you mean?"

"You criticized every word I wrote."

"Is that what it felt like?" Jonathan asked.

"It's true. You pointed out each little thing I did wrong, and told me I should do it differently," I said.

Jonathan exhaled as though I had knocked the wind out of him. "I hadn't even realized. I hate it when my editor does that to me."

"That's happened to you?"

"Are you kidding? I tell him all the time to start with the positive stuff, *then* he can critique the rest! But he feels like the good stuff speaks for itself, and just skips that and heads straight for the things I need to improve. It makes me question every key I hit, which is a good thing in the end, but I lose more hair every time I sit down to work. No one said writing was easy, though, huh?"

"I thought you'd know how to do it by now."

He rubbed his eyes and said, "I'm sorry I didn't tell you first how impressed I was, and am, with your interviews. I like how you turned your questions and answers into stories, rather than just list the Q&A."

"Thanks," I said. "Finally."

Jonathan chuckled, making his dimples grow deeper. "I love to write, Addy. But that doesn't mean it's not a hard thing to do. I edit and recraft the same work until I'm sure I'll never get it right. Then, somehow, finally, I'm sitting in front of a finished piece. And then I send it to my editor."

"I thought once you learned how to write, you

could sit down and it would just pour out," I said.

Jonathan smiled and shook his head. "I wish!"

"You know," I said, "even if we had writing in common, we don't need to write the same stupid things, do we?"

"No," he agreed. "We can write entirely different stupid things."

The doorbell rang just as I was about to snag the bathroom. Mom said, "Can you get that please, Addy? I'll shower first, then you can go."

I ran down and opened the door to find Jackie holding out an envelope.

"What's that?"

Jackie said, "It's the article on Jonathan. My mom thought you guys might like an extra copy."

"What article?" I peeked in the envelope.

"The one you were supposed to be in . . . you know, the day we went to the diner. It came out pretty good," Jackie said. "Though I don't know how, since she never got to talk to you." I made a face and she wrinkled her nose at me. "The whole thing's about how he interviewed all these grieving families who lost a loved one to cancer," Jackie told me. "I liked the part about how hard it was to keep his mind clear so he could write their story, and not think about his own."

"His own what?" I asked.

"*Story.* You know, how his wife died of cancer

249

when she was only twenty-four. He'd be writing about these people and start thinking about—"

"I didn't know she had cancer," I said. I wondered if he had ever cried at night like my mom. Well, like she used to before they met.

Jackie asked, "Can you come over? I want you to see my whole outfit before the dance."

I looked up the stairs, but knew if I left the house I'd be grounded until I was forty-three-and-a-half years old. "Nah, we're leaving for the Platinum Pencil thing as soon as everyone's ready. Jonathan has to be there a little early. Take a picture, though, okay?"

"Are you kidding? My dad has like, seven cameras all ready, just in case one goes on the fritz. See ya."

I went back upstairs and flopped onto my bed. I opened the envelope and started reading the article. It was all about the Platinum Pencil award and how Jonathan was winning for his series called "Cancer's Other Victims: Families and Grief in America." There was a time line that showed how it'd taken him almost two years just to talk to everyone. He had finally learned to cope with his

250

wife's death, and then he lived through it again, over and over, every time he interviewed a new family. Some had lost lots of people. But even though the whole series was about grief, having hope was the message.

One woman had lost her father, her husband, and her son all in one year. I read on, and it was Madame Jeannie, from Lovely Ladies Lingerie! She said the way she deals with it is she looks for the good things in life, and making other people happy. She said, "I embraced my grief, gave it its due, and then I had to move on. When they were alive, I did what I could to take care of them. I loved them, and then I had to let them go. I look forward to the joyful things in my life now, like my daughter's wedding. That's what you have to do. Keep living life."

After my shower, I went downstairs, my new blue dress swishing and shushing as I took each step. It seemed to whisper, "Keep living life . . . keep living life. . . ." Madame Jeannie had worse luck than I've had, and she didn't blame some old family curse.

Maybe Jonathan wouldn't be so bad to have

around. If I could end up friends with Marsha Pittel, *anything* is possible. She hadn't taken my place as Jackie's best friend. It turned out she's an *additional* friend. Maybe it was the same with Jonathan. He couldn't take Dad's place.

No way.

Not even close.

But maybe he could be, like, an *additional* dad.

"Here are the pearls, just like I promised," Mom said, looping the strand around my neck and clicking the clasp shut. She put her hands on my shoulders, and turned me around to face her. Her eyes filled with tears as she looked at me. "You are just stunning. Daddy would've loved seeing you all dressed up like this."

"You look pretty good yourself, Mom."

"You think?" Her dress was elegant, but funky, too. It was old—no, *vintage*—with little sparkly sequins all over it. It went down to the calf, with tiny beads dangling from the hem, the collar, and sleeves.

"Yeah. You look excellent." She linked her arm

through mine, and we walked to the driveway where Jonathan and Nicky were already waiting.

"I'm glad we're going in your car, Jonathan," I said as we all got in and clicked into our seatbelts. "It's way nicer."

"Gee, thanks," my mother said, pretending to be hurt.

"Well, your backseat always has some combo of a half-eaten Power Bar, hair scrunchies, empty water bottles, and all the school flyers we bring home that you don't want to read."

"I only toss that stuff in the back temporarily."

Nicky and I looked at each other and raised our eyebrows.

As he pulled onto the main road, Jonathan asked, "So how long *is* 'temporarily,' anyway?" My mom gave his shoulder a little shove. "What?" he said. "It's not my fault your car has looked like that since Christmas. Christmas, circa 1932!"

"He has a point, Mom," I said.

"Addy, do you remember me telling you that everyone in the industry will be there tonight?"

Jonathan asked, looking at me in the rearview mirror. "If it's a literary magazine, they'd have gotten a table for their top editors."

"Oh yeah, I do. That's cool."

"Kids' magazines too, I mean. Including your formerly 'favorite journal in the whole universe.'"

My mom leaned toward him and said, "No, it's called her 'favorite magazine on the entire planet.'"

"Mom," I said, leaning forward, "it's okay. Close enough."

Jonathan said, "I know the editor there. Would you like me to introduce you?"

I sat up straight. "You know the editor of *Chanticleer*?"

"Yep."

Whoa. What if the editor told Jonathan about my entry? Now that everything had changed, I really didn't want him to see what I had done. Sheesh clabeesh, when would I learn? How many times did I have to hurt someone before I *really* gave up writing? And now, it would be published when I won, and if Jonathan got upset, it was possible he would actually move out. Then my mom would be hurt, too. What had I been thinking?

I said to Jonathan, "Definitely." I knew what I would do. I'd meet the editor and explain that he should not publish my comic. It was my only chance to avoid another disaster.

When we got there and started walking toward the hotel, Nicky and Jonathan trotted ahead, since we were running a little late and the reporters were waiting for the star of the show.

My mom was looking at me all glowy and everything.

I asked, "What?"

"Nothing."

"No, Mom, what?"

"What's with you and Jonathan? You two were practically friendly in the car."

"Nothing's *with* us, Mom. You don't have to get all gushy on me." She was still looking at me with goo-goo eyes, so I said, "He's definitely never going to be my dad, but maybe I don't hate him, okay?"

"Well, that's a start, anyway."

The Platinum Pencil awards were held in a big fancy hotel, with lots of ballrooms and conference centers and all that. Marble floors and walls were lit up by gigantic crystal chandeliers. People in fancy outfits were having cocktails in the lobby before going into the ballroom where the ceremony would be held. We found Jonathan next to a man with red hair and a beard to match. He wore a checkered bow tie and was talking and waving his hands all over the place. His arms swept around as I walked up behind him, and I ducked just in time.

Jonathan said, "Oh, here she is," and gestured to me. "Addy, I'd like you to meet Shaun Glazier. Shaun, this is Addy McMahon, Cassie's daughter."

I stuck my hand out to shake and the man grabbed it and said, "Addy McMahon? I know that name." He stroked his beard and looked up toward the chandeliers. "Where've I heard that name before?"

Jonathan said, "A lot of people know her from her wonderful and unique interviews for *The Seely Times*, her school paper. Do you have children in our district?"

256

"No, that's not it. I think—wait!" The guy hadn't let go of my hand yet, and it felt like he was going to shake my arm right out of the socket. "Did you submit a graphic story to the *Chanticleer* contest?"

Jonathan looked at me with surprise. I couldn't meet his eye.

I asked Mr. Glazier, "How did you know that?"

Jonathan said, "This is the man I told you I'd introduce you to. I'm sorry, didn't I say that? He's the editor-in-chief of your 'favorite magazine on the entire planet.'" Luckily, at that moment someone called Jonathan away, and my mother and Nicky went with him, leaving me alone with Mr. Glazier.

"How could you remember my submission? Don't you get hundreds of entries?" But I had a sinking feeling I had the answer. He knew who I was because I had won. I had actually won, and now I wasn't so sure I wanted to. It would be "The Mental Adventures of Jackie White" all over again. Not only that, but I will have ruined my mom's chance at happiness.

All this time I'd been thinking of us as a wound,

and Jonathan as the sting-y stuff. But what if he were the Band-Aid? Maybe I was cursed after all.

No. No curse.

Just *me* making another huge mistake.

Mr. Glazier laughed. "Actually, we get thousands of entries. But only one was a graphic story. It was really quite wonderful and got us all talking."

My stomach sank. I couldn't believe I had my fingers crossed, but this time hoping I *wouldn't* win. "So, then, I won? Is there any way you can change your mind? I mean, isn't there someone else who—"

"I'm sorry to interrupt you, Addy. But—can you keep a secret? At least until the announcement tomorrow morning?" When I nodded, he continued. "No, you did not win."

Even though I didn't want to hurt Jonathan anymore, and especially my mother, I was shocked. "*What?* Why not?"

"There are contest rules which need to be followed, for legal reasons. We weren't accepting illustrations in any form, regardless of how enchanting they might be. However, as I said, your entry was

258

intriguing, and my staff and I are now considering a new feature for the magazine, and we'd like to talk to you about it further. As long as it's okay with your folks, would you be interested?"

All I could think about, after finding out I hadn't won, was how relieved I felt. I didn't mess up . . . finally. Mr. Glazier was looking at me, waiting for an answer. "Uh, sure, that would be great."

"Fine, fine, then. I'll get your number from Jonathan. Have fun tonight!"

"Wait, Mr. Glazier? What do you do with the submissions that didn't win?" I had a horrible vision of getting mine back and not being able to destroy it fast enough.

"I'm sorry, Addy," Mr. Glazier said. "We can't return anything. There are just too many stories. We have to recycle it all. No one else will ever see that particular comic." He winked at me and disappeared into the crowd.

Everyone was still hovering around, talking and congratulating Jonathan and asking him questions about his interviews. I walked over to hear what people were saying and realized I had never even read them.

As I got closer, a woman in a beautiful red gown rushed up to Jonathan and started shaking his hand like crazy. "Oh, oh my gosh. I cannot believe I'm meeting you. I'm a huge fan of your work." Then she blushed, and said, "You *are* Jonathan Waddey, right? I mean, I'm not making a fool of myself to the wrong person?"

Jonathan smiled. "Yes, I am, but it's pronounced Wad*day*, even though it's spelled *W-A-D-D-E-Y*."

"Oh," said the woman, "you mean with an accent, like French?"

I started to laugh, and she turned to me.

"Is this your daughter?"

"This is Addy," Jonathan said.

The woman leaned toward me and whispered, "Lucky for you it's *not* pronounced the way I said it, am I right, hon?" I looked from her to Jonathan and back to the woman. She said, "Addy Wad*dey* is so much nicer than Addy Waddey!"

Jonathan must've seen the look of horror streak

across my face and rushed the lady away to introduce her to his editor.

Addy Waddey? I'd always keep my father's name, of course, but boy, would Marsha love this when I told her!

Nicky had gone off to look for our table, which was supposed to be next to the stage. I found him and sat down, and Mom and Jonathan soon followed. There were tons of tables, and every one had ten or fifteen people at it. If I did the math, which I never would, there were probably hundreds of people. And they were all there to honor Jonathan's writing.

"Hey, Addy," Nicky whispered, "check this out! I got stuff!" He held out a black canvas tote bag with a big fancy pencil silk-screened in silver. Something looked funny about the pencil, but I couldn't figure out what it was. I looked around and saw the same bag hanging on the back of every chair. I turned to grab mine, but then the lights dimmed and everyone hushed.

A bunch of speakers started going up to present

honors before the main award, which was the Platinum Pencil. One woman received an honor for nonfiction writing in both the children's as well as the adult category. She'd written about illiteracy, and the different ways kids and grown-ups dealt with not being able to read.

Another went to the podium accompanied by some music that sounded like cartoon sound effects, and it turned out he'd won the humor award. The funniest part of his speech was that it was so serious. He went on a long time about how comedy never got any respect, even in the movie business, and gave some statistics of how rare it was for humorous movies to win an Academy Award.

It was pretty cool to be in the middle of all these actual writers, and even though most of the speeches were interesting, I started thinking about how it must feel to know that other journalists respected what you wrote. I thought about how all these people got their start, and wondered if any of them had ever written for *Chanticleer*. I pretended I was the one going up there to accept an award. I saw myself climbing the steps to the podium.

Mr. Glazier was at the next table, making a little phone out of his hand and pointing at me. I wondered what his staff was considering adding to the magazine, and why they would need to talk to me. Then I realized something else. I hadn't even been thinking about losing the contest . . . that was a shocker! I was sad I didn't win, of course, but it was really great I hadn't ruined everything again.

More people gave speeches, and I listened off and on while they spoke. I was looking around the room at all the fancy dresses when they started serving dinner. It was chicken a la something, and tasted like a doll I had when I was five. Nicky, of course, thought it was delicious.

Finally it was time for Jonathan's award. His editor got up and started talking about him. He told about how Jonathan had lost his young wife to cancer, and then he said, "His interviews with cancer patients and their families was the most moving and thought-provoking I have read, bar none. Although it was personal, Jonathan's grief informed his writing

263

and elevated his work to the finest example of award-winning journalism." He paused, and the room was completely silent. He took a breath, held out his arm toward our table, and announced, "Ladies and gentlemen, I give you Jonathan Waddey!"

Everyone jumped to their feet and clapped like crazy. Jonathan went up to the podium and held up his hands to quiet the room. He started his speech by thanking the people who'd helped him bring his work to a whole new level, including his editor. Then he said my mom's name.

". . . and if Cassie hadn't come into my life at that point, I probably would have given up on writing, not to mention life, altogether. Thank goodness she was one of my earliest interviews, because . . ."

Whoa. I didn't know that's how they met! I missed the next part of the speech while I tried to figure out when that must've been. Then I heard my own name.

". . . because of Nicky and Addy, Cassie's children. This series would never have been written had it not been for their father, and the sadness they experienced at his passing. So this is not my award alone. I truly cannot take responsibility for the success of the series, as it rests on the grief-stricken shoulders of all the families who have shared a tragedy."

After it was all over and we went home, Jonathan came into my room with a package wrapped in purple, with flowers cut from construction paper glued all over it, and a big red bow. My mom stood behind him, and I could tell the flowers were her contribution.

"I was so hyper-focused," he said, looking down at the package in his hands. "I felt bad that you thought I'd given you such harsh critiques of your work, and I wanted to make it up to you. He fiddled around with the bow until it was about to come undone. "Addy, I wanted to prove to you that I believed in your creative talents, and so, I hope you don't mind, and your mother said she thought it would be okay when she gave me the original, I still have it, so don't worry, and besides . . ."

"Just give it to her!" My mom said.

He handed me the present. I sat on the edge of my bed, untied the bow the rest of the way, and pulled it off. I turned the box over and slid my finger under where the tape was holding the paper together and snapped it open. When I lifted the lid and saw what was lying nestled in tissue paper, I gasped.

Inside was a slick-looking booklet. It was printed just like a real comic book, in full color, and looked exactly like one you'd buy in a store. I saw that Jonathan had added some type to the cover. It read:

The Dragon Knight
By Addy and Evan McMahon

"Wow, Jonathan. I never . . . I wouldn't have thought . . . you really didn't . . ." I sighed. "Thanks."

Jonathan grinned, and I smiled back. My mom was beaming, and it was obvious it killed her to leave, but she had to put Nicky to bed.

"I never actually read it, you know," Jonathan said, taking the chair from my desk to face me. We sat knee to knee. I looked up from the comic, still cradled in the box. He added, "I wanted to be careful not to invade your privacy."

I plucked the booklet out of its nest and opened it to a drawing I remembered struggling over. "See this angle? I couldn't figure out how to make the kid look like he was really sliding down the mountain, so my dad told me about how artists use photographs sometimes as reference. That means they refer to it to see how it should be done."

I told him how comics are really like frames of a movie, each pushing the action along. I described all the ways you can speed up the pace, or stop it dead, just by making a character face a certain direction. I explained how I like to use different drawing tricks to add drama and showed him some rejected sketches and compared them to the final ones.

After a long time, Jonathan asked me to read him the story, and when I finished, he had questions about every panel and every illustration.

He didn't give any tips.

It took me a long time to fall asleep, but when I did,

I dreamed I went into a store and all these kids were there to buy my comic book. When I opened my eyes the next morning, I sent Jackie an e-mail to call as soon as she got up, and went to bring the phone into my room. I slid back under my covers, and gazed at the booklet some more. I thought I was going to wear it out, I stared at it so much. The phone rang and I looked at the caller ID, hoping it was Jackie. It was.

"Thanks for not waking me with a call, even though my computer yelled out "YOU'VE GOT MAIL" when your post came through. Man, it's early. So how was it?"

"Jackie, you won't believe this!" I told her the whole story.

"And you're not even upset about losing the contest? Who *are* you?"

I said, "I know, weird, huh?"

"Freakishly," Jackie said. "I told you he wasn't that bad."

"He isn't that bad, but that still doesn't mean he's going to be my dad."

"Doy. You are so demented."

"Am not."

"Are too."

"So, don't you have anything to tell me?" I asked. I could practically hear her blushing over the phone line.

"It was so much fun, Addy. But we missed you. Ezra picked me up with Mr. Samuels and he and my dad made us take about four million pictures. I'll show you later. He got a haircut and everything, Addy."

"Who? Your dad?"

"No! Ezra!"

"Ez? You are kidding me."

"He buzzed it."

"Get *out*," I said.

"Stay *in*. Anyway, I'll tell you about it later, maybe after I sleep ten or eleven more hours?"

"No problem," I said. "That'll give me time to finish the rest of Jonathan's interviews. They printed them all up in one bound copy and gave it to every-one." After we hung up, I fingered the elegant silk screen of the silver pencil on the tote until I finally realized what was weird about it. Here was this fancy and perfect pencil, except for the eraser, which was worn down to a little nubby stub. I smiled, remembering what Jonathan had said about how hard it was to revise his work. The abused eraser stump was a good way to show that even famous, grown-up writers made mistakes. And I guess that's okay, as long as you try to make it right in the end.

I settled back and started reading Madame Jeannie's interview. I got to the same quote that was in the newspaper article on Jonathan. Her line, "keep living life," echoed in my brain.

That's when I got the idea. I jumped off the bed and went to my desk. I opened the bottom drawer and looked into the dimness.

"Put something beautiful in it, Addy. Something that will remind you of me, no matter what happens," my father had said.

I picked up the frame and brought it into the light. It was covered with dust. My tights from the night before were on the floor in a heap. I grabbed them and wiped the frame clean. I snapped the back off and put it on my bed. I lay my published comic into the opening, placed the back on, and clipped the fasteners closed. It was a perfect fit.

I set the story my father and I created together, protected in the frame he made for me, on my shelf where I could see it every day.

THIRD, MADAME JEANNIE IS GOING TO FRAME MY FIRST *CHANTICLEER* PIECE (AFTER ALL, IT **IS** ABOUT HER), AND HANG IT IN THE NEW LOVELY LADIES **SALON** (**NOT** NEAR THE BRAS!) PLUS, SHE GAVE US ALL **FREE** LOVELY LADIES MAKEOVERS!

ENTER STEVE GECK.
AN EDITOR WITH THE
UNCANNY ABILITY TO DISTILL
AN ENTIRE CONCEPT INTO
A SINGLE WORD.
IT WAS THIS TALENT THAT
CAUSED CEREBRAL
CHAIN REACTIONS,
EMANCIPATING UNEXPECTED
IDEAS THAT BROUGHT
THIS BOOK
TO NEW LEVELS
WITH EVERY REVISION.

RUBY DAVIS, AKA THE YOUNGEST
CRITIQUER, MADE OBSERVATIONS WELL
BEYOND HER YEARS, CATCHING LITTLE
THINGS THAT MAKE THE DIFFERENCE
BETWEEN BELIEVING A CHARACTER AND
TOSSING A BOOK ASIDE IN FRUSTRATION.
HER SUGGESTIONS HELPED MAKE THIS
STORY CLICK INTO PLACE.

AT CRUCIAL MOMENTS OF
DEJECTION AND REJECTION,
BENNY DAVIS BESTOWED
THE KINDEST AND MOST
ENERGIZING OF COMPLIMENTS:

JERRY DAVIS, IN ADDITION TO BEING
BLESSED WITH DASHING GOOD LOOKS
AND SKILLED FANCY FOOTWORK
ON THE DANCE FLOOR . . .

I'M A GOOD
WRITER BECAUSE
OF **YOU**,
MOM.

. . . KNOWS HOW
TO MAKE
EVERYTHING POSSIBLE.